Daniel Lowe

About the Author

JANE MCCAFFERTY grew up in Wilmington, Delaware, and received her B.A. from the University of Delaware and her M.F.A. from the University of Pittsburgh. She is the author of the novel *One Heart*. Her previous collection of stories, *Director of the World*, won the Drue Heinz Literature Prize, and she's had six stories listed in *Best American Short Stories*. She has also been awarded a Pushcart Prize and an NEA fellowship for her fiction. McCafferty lives in Pittsburgh, Pennsylvania, and teaches at Carnegie Mellon University.

ALSO BY JANE McCAFFERTY

One Heart
Director of the World & Other Stories

THANK YOU FOR THE MUSIC

Stories

JANE McCAFFERTY

Perennial

An Imprint of HarperCollins*Publishers*

HarperCollins books may be purchased for educational, business, or sales promotional use. For information please write: Special Markets Department, HarperCollins Publishers Inc., 10 East 53rd Street, New York, NY 10022.

FIRST EDITION

Designed by Elias Haslanger

Library of Congress Cataloging-in-Publication Data is available upon request.

ISBN 0-06-056453-9

04 05 06 07 08 ❖/RRD 10 9 8 7 6 5 4 3 2 1

THESE STORIES HAVE APPEARED IN THE FOLLOWING PUBLICATIONS

"Family on Ice" in *Glimmer Train*

"The Pastor's Brother" forthcoming in *Iowa Review*

"Guiding Light" in *Glimmer Train*

"Berna's Place" in *Witness*

"Brother to Brother" in *Fugue*

"You Could Never Love the Clown I Love" in *Gulf Stream*

"The Dog Who Saved Her" in *Witness*

"So Long, Marianne" in *West Branch*

"Elizabeth Tines" in *Heart Quarterly*

"Stadium Hearts" in *Story*

"Embraced" in *Epoch*

"Thank You for the Music" forthcoming in *Witness*

FOR MY BROTHERS, DAVID AND MATT

Acknowledgments

Deep gratitude goes to my agent, Nicole Aragi, my editor, Marjorie Braman, and to Daniel Lowe, who generously read and commented on these stories first.

To all those at HarperCollins who worked in various ways to turn the manuscript into a book: thanks for that labor.

I'd also like to thank readers Daniel Arp, Jane Bernstein, Kristin Kovacic, and Bill Deasy for their helpful comments on some of these stories; Paul Ingram and John Evans, for working hard to launch my novel; and Jim Schley, steadfast reader and priceless pen pal through the decades.

Special thanks to Peter Stine, whose always excellent *Witness* helped to inspire many of these and other stories, and to all my family, old teachers, students, and increasingly dear friends, old and new, near and far, whose humbling influence is both irreplaceable and impossible to measure.

Contents

Family on Ice 1

The Pastor's Brother 19

Guiding Light 43

Berna's Place 59

Light of Lucy 91

Brother to Brother 103

You Could Never Love the Clown I Love 109

The Dog Who Saved Her 115

Dear Mister Springsteen 129

So Long, Marianne 141

Elizabeth Tines 153

Stadium Hearts 169

Embraced 183

Thank You for the Music 201

Thank You for the Music

FAMILY ON ICE

NOT THAT YOU ASKED, but I'm an X-ray tech going to night school for anthropology.

I have a daughter, who is seven, and spends a lot of time with her father in the suburbs.

I have the kind of loneliness that makes me sit too close, on purpose, to strange men on buses. Men who smell good, who read books, whose shoes are not too shiny, not too scuffed.

I have not learned to appreciate solitude.

And yes, I know this attitude has long been out of vogue. All the magazines have headlines that shout SINGLE? CELE-BRATE! Everyone seems to talk about being a *woman warrior* who works out six times a week. It makes me want to take up smoking again, and sit in a bar all afternoon the way I did in my twenties.

In my present social life that matters, I'm the third wheel. The other two wheels are Henry and Lydia, and wouldn't you know it, Henry loves Lydia and *Lydia loves life*, art, sports, and perhaps, though we're not sure yet, Henry. He's enjoying the toying, delicious, piercing pleasure-pain of not knowing. She calls him Henri, like she's French, not in a pretentious way, but in a way that makes you recognize her humor, her great accent, and her big vision of the world, like Paris is always in the air even though it's Pittsburgh. She wears a black beret at an angle you might have to call jaunty. She would never eat cheese doodles for dinner with a loud TV like some people I know; she'd prepare thick split pea soup, eat quietly with classical music on the radio, stare into her small backyard, where she once kept a warren of little white rabbits who slept on her couch when it was cold. She is the sort of woman who always thinks before speaking, and who never says "um" or "ya know." She wears bright silk scarves tied around her head, and is constantly clearing her eyes with drops of Visine, her only addiction. If her eyes get any clearer, any bluer, any more beautiful with wide-eyed—what is it? wonder?—they'll crack like windows in a hurricane.

And now she's invited the two of us to go ice skating with her entire family. Did I mention that I love Henry? *Henry the divorced insomniac*, the owner of a used bookstore? Did I mention that the very idea of a family that goes ice skating together is beyond my ken? And that's the first time in my life I've used the word "ken," so sorry for being fancy, as my grandmother used to say.

She also used to holler, "It's always funny, 'til somebody loses an eye!"

She's dead now, like so many others in my family, but even if they were alive they wouldn't be caught dead on skates. Most of them managed to fall on their asses wearing shoes. Many of them would've considered me heroic for holding down a job, and raising a kid. "How do you do it?" they'd ask, if they weren't dead.

I have to envy Lydia, whose mother used to play the clarinet each morning to rouse her children from slumber, whose handsome father, a minor-league baseball player, decided he wanted to learn to quilt, so took a quilting class in Bloomfield with several old Italian women, and made something beautiful to hang on the wall. I have to envy Lydia with a passion I believe warps my soul. Nobody *drank to excess* in her family, much less *did heroin,* nobody ever *threw slabs* of Christmas roast beef at the ceiling or drove a car through a living room wall, or disappeared for seven years, or became a transvestite (nothing against transvestites), and you can see this by looking at them—physical beauty, yes, but somehow quaint and New Englandy, like people in old photographs: Observing their profiles you feel the romance and heirloomy fullness of their story, the certainty that generations from now, their children's children will say, "And that's why I play the clarinet—it's a tradition, you see—"

Tradition! It's very true some people still have them, and not just farmers. I keep thinking I need to invent some traditions for my daughter.

Her name is Rhonda and she's never seen her aunts. One of them has been telling me for eight years she'd love to see me if it weren't for "the troubles." Like she's in Ireland! My other sister and I are simply not speaking for reasons I couldn't bear to bare right now. Rhonda did see my parents before they died, but what can a kid say to a three-hundred-pound woman who smokes her way through lung cancer? What can a kid say to a dry drunk so mortified by emotion he kept his heart in a glass cage up in the attic? Or somewhere. I was grateful to them for dying. They'd died a long time before their real deaths anyhow. And I didn't want my kid looking at them too closely here in the age of genes-are-us. Instead I make up lies about them. "Your grandmother was an excellent seamstress, and *quite* the muckraker. Sympathy for the

Underdog was her middle name." "Your grandfather was valedictorian and a friend to all animals." I buy old photos in antique stores and educate her about her ancestors. I pick the most interestingly dignified photos I can find, and all she can say is, "Why didn't they smile back in the olden days?"

Anyhow, she's lately spending most of her time with her father and his girlfriend, Sandy Meg. Since Sandy Meg is loaded with stockbroker money, when my daughter comes home she's always got several new Barbies—the kind in lavish ball gowns I could never buy her. I benefit from this, since it's clear Rhonda feels a little guilty about preferring Sandy Meg's bubbly wealth and wry electric company to my own. This guilt makes her more affectionate and charming to be with. She pretends to be interested in the gorilla book I bought her last year. She cleans her room without my having to ask. In her seven-year-old eyes I see pity when I try to tell her I think there might be more to life than Barbies. Poor Mom, the brown eyes say, don't you get it? And then a kind of resignation sets in: Oh well, so I have a mother who doesn't understand how sparkly life can be.

Even at age seven she knows there are worse things.

It's a little complex watching someone you desperately love trying to impress someone they desperately love. I sit there in the restaurant called Champs with Henry and Lydia around a little table, and when Henry starts talking about all his work with Habitat for Humanity, it's clear to me he's doing this so Lydia's bleeding heart will swell, and when she seems a little bored with his description of drywall, I secretly feel happy. (What kind of love is it where you're rooting for your loved one to fail? Why am I so comfortable with the conventional selfishness of this desire?) I try to steer his attention my way— hey, Henry, over here, I *love* drywall stories, my eyes plead—

but of course he's looking at the Visine Queen in action and thinking what next to say—did she know he used to live down the street from Arlo Guthrie? That gets her. She blinks back the excess eyedrops. She's an Arlo Guthrie fan! Bingo. Let's hope Arlo doesn't get Huntingtons, she says. Yeah, man. She loves "Coming into Los Angeles." She remembers her hippie cousin playing it for her when she was eight.

The two of them are off and running, and they love Woody Guthrie too, and Lydia says she cried the first time she heard Springsteen sing "This Land Is Your Land," and why can't that be the national anthem? Henry says he can't believe it—he's always wondered that himself! He sounds pathetic now, like a me-too boy, not a thirty-five-year-old insomniac bookstore owner, and if Lydia would recoil a bit I'd have to put my hand on his knee to comfort him.

I have known and loved him now for over two long years. I bought him warm cinnamon buns each morning for four months after another woman broke his heart—a red-haired nurse who'd published a parody on those books of affirmations. In the red-haired nurse's book, the affirmations were all like "Today I will finally embrace the fact that I am a complete loser and will remain as such." It's true, she was brilliant, and I too was half in love with her, and part of what bonded Henry to me was the empathy I felt when he lost this genius.

I feel for him still. I know he is the son of a foul-tempered autocrat and a woman who chased neighborhood children from her lawn with a broom. My heart breaks a little seeing his effort in the face of Lydia's reserve.

He glances over at me once. Contained in such moments is the possibility that he actually loves me, and simply doesn't know it yet.

I sigh, move my body protectively toward him. But then something barely perceptible shifts in the atmosphere.

Lydia and he are suddenly having a moment.

They're having eye contact where you can feel a kind of sticky rainbow arching between them.

I take my body back, and look out the window of the little coffee shop. I avoid the eyes of the white-haired woman hunched in her black coat, standing alone on the corner as if she's suddenly forgotten her name, where she's going, or where the hell she's been. Why is she looking at me?

Christmas Eve. My daughter is spending it with Dad and Sandy Meg. We've taken a bus to the corner of Oak Ridge Lane, then walked into the canned air of a cul-de-sac. I miss my car, but it's not time, money-wise, to get it fixed yet, and Rhonda thinks riding the bus is thrilling, especially the golden ones. I kiss her good-bye at the suburban curb in the powder-pink hooded coat Sandy Meg's mother bought her. The kind with a furry hood that frames her fat little face so you have to kiss it more than usual. My ex-husband calls out from a second-story window, "Merry Christmas," but before I can return the greeting he appears to have ducked. The window is empty. He was this way when I was married to him too—said things and disappeared before I could think how to respond. In the windows they have blue candles. When I was a child I burned my tongue on one of those things. "Don't let her lick the candles, okay?" I call, and Sandy Meg nods and squints. Did you just say something about licking the candles? she wants to say, but won't. "Thanks, Sandy," I say, because I can't bring myself to call her Sandy Meg out loud. "Merry Christmas," she calls, with a certain droll irony in her voice that I appreciate. She might be rich, but she's a thinker. She's got a cold eye peeled on the familiar little drama we're caught in.

♬

Later Henry and I take the bus to Lydia's. He's dressed in a charcoal-gray sweater and faded jeans, construction boots and a pea coat. He's got his broadly sympathetic bookstore-owner face well scrubbed and shaved. I refuse to look at his curly haired beauty—though I can feel his eyes seeking mine—and in order to avoid his musings about whether Lydia will like the pink suede gloves he's bought her, I chat with the bus driver, who tells me he collected a hundred coats for the poor this year. He took the hundred coats to a shelter. He felt damn good about it, and Christmas was in his heart now, "unlike all the other years when I was a selfish bastard."

"A hundred coats," Henry says. "That's so tangible. I like that."

"Next year I'm going to do the same," I say.

"Why wait until next year?" Henry says. "Let's do it this coming week. We can go out to the suburbs and collect coats all day long." (He's the sort who will actually do this.)

"Okay."

"Seriously, me and you, next week. Coat collectors."

I love when Henry makes plans with me this way.

The bus driver doesn't answer, and is quiet the rest of the ride, like maybe he's a little mad that we're stealing his idea.

"Merry Christmas," we say, stepping down into the night.

"Uh-huh," he says.

In Lydia's house we sip cider in the attic, where Lydia still has her childhood table and chairs and tea set and toys in a little alcove. It's her idea to take us up there, and Henry, of course, is overcome with tenderness and awe, for here he sits where his love once sat as a child thirty years ago. I feel like a giant, like I could bust the chair in two if I shift my weight. Maybe I secretly want to break everything I see. It wouldn't be the first time. I sip my cider and watch the two of them. Lydia's telling him about the imaginary world she and her sister inhabited up here. They had imaginary friends, Missy

Looler and Tina, who were blue and tiny and wore clothing made of flowers. Missy Looler and Tina, Lydia says, were still here in spirit, and she asks Henry and me to get very, very quiet, so we could feel or hear these tiny blue spirits (only Lydia could make this poetic little request without seeming saccharine), and wouldn't you know it, Henry gets wide-eyed, Henry, who is thirty-five years old, becomes intimate with both Missy Looler and Tina! He looks across the table at Lydia as if he is willing himself to be five again, inserting himself into her own childhood memory, smiling, his whole body one long hush of blue fairies until Lydia finally says, "See what I mean?" and Henry says, "Missy Looler was on my neck," and Lydia smiles and then looks at me as if about to say, "Did you feel them?" but, to her credit, says nothing. She must have sensed that I was the uncomfortable giantess in a memory I could not and did not want to enter. Missy Looler was not on my neck, nor was her cohort, Tina, but now they would be stuck in my head forever.

"Shall we go downstairs?" I say.

I'm sorry to say that everyone down there was a little too interesting for their own good, just like Lydia's father. My patience was wearing thin. Have you ever found extremely interesting people to be tiresome and boring? Their finest qualities—intelligence, charm, deep, broad vision and experience of the world—sometimes these are the biggest yawns of all. One of the beautiful sisters had lived in Portugal. She is generously articulate with her Portugal stories, inserting Portuguese words into her talk. She is also a bright-scarf woman, like Lydia. Another sister has played the harp since she was nine, and it shows. Beautifully. She makes the aunt in the roses shawl weep by the Christmas tree with its tasteful gold lights. "O Holy Night," played the harp in the candlelit corner of the wreathy room—naturally she would play that one, that being the prettiest, most tasteful Christmas song. She has yellow hair, it hangs down, the little nephews with their pocket video games worship at her feet, a baby cries and is ushered into the other room. The weeping aunt, Lydia whispers, lost her husband to cancer three years ago. They'd been best friends all their lives. Thick, family compassion for her fills the room; she looks up with her eyes filled with tears and love, and with the knowledge that life is good and worth living, that she's part of a tribe. Lydia's mother picks up her clarinet, and I walk out onto the back porch as if I were still a smoker. It's cold out here. Nice. A person could close their eyes and feel they were anywhere.

When I look up I see a wiry old guy who may be sixty standing beyond the porch in the backyard, moonlit, wearing a green parka, his face lined and his hair under the hood a silver-white shock, as they say. He has that craggy old-time rumpled journalist look.

"What kinda individ-jull are you to leave a party like that?" he says, and cocks his head toward the house.

"What kind of individual are you to stand in the backyard all alone?"

"I'm the family bum."

Something in my heart swells, as if he's told me, I'm your prince, your dream come true.

"What makes you think you're the family bum?" I say. I walk outside to join him. The night is a dark, cold relief.

"I hate Christmas, and I hate cozy rooms filled with loving people. My brother is especially on my last nerves tonight."

"Is your brother Lydia's father? The handsome baseball-playing quilt maker?"

Somehow I manage to imbue those words with just enough scorn. I can see the family bum move wholeheartedly into his own face for a moment of real connection, and then retreat again.

"That's him," he says. "Catalogue man." He looks up at the thin black sky.

"I thought this family was perfect," I say.

"Oh, it is. And I'm part of that perfection. You're old enough to know you need someone like me around to know how perfect you are, aren't you?"

He turns to survey my face. He looks thoughtful.

"I'm plenty old enough," I say, and he smiles, inexplicably. It's a tired smile, one that probably belongs to someone else, some woman in his memory whom I've evoked.

"Hey!" a voice calls from the kitchen door. It's Lydia. "Come on, you two! It's time to go skating!"

Somehow she deepens our backyard bond a notch by referring to us as *you two,* as if the sight of us there in the darkness makes intuitive sense to her. The family bum takes my arm and escorts me through the dark toward the door.

This fills me with good humor until I step inside and see Henry's face. For a moment I consider shaking him by the shoulders, shouting into his face, "I love you and this game has got to stop!"

"Where were you?" he asks, all concerned and flushed in the cheek. His worried brown eyes search my own. I shrug and smile. "Outside."

"Oh," he says, still looking at me, then looking over at the family bum, who is opening a bottle of beer. It's just this kind of response that keeps me hopeful as a stupid girl with a crush, hope that keeps me wondering whether really, deep down, it's me he loves.

Lydia might very well be an infatuation. In her pink suede gloves she is laughing now. If she keeps him at bay long enough, he'll get weary. And I'll be there, as Michael Jackson sang when he was eight.

She ushers us all toward the front door. Caravan time. We're off to the pond. Lydia's brother carries an enormous box of skates for all. The little ones are yelping for joy.

Folding chairs are lined by the edge of the pond, here where the moon is low over the pines, where the kids in fat snow-suits ring out Bart Simpson's version of "Rudolf," and Henry is beside me in the cold night, so close when he turns to speak his breath warms my cheek, and my body is fired with dire restraint. Lydia calls us over. "Come on, I got skates over here old enough to be your mother!" I look out over the smooth pond and my heart quickens. I haven't been skating since age twelve. I'd been in love then, too, with a boy named Mickey Seems, who hadn't liked me much—I wasn't popular—but my friend had paid him two bucks to go "couple-skating" with me while they blasted Paul McCartney's "My Love"; I grew so nervous my ankles kept folding inward. Resentful Mickey Seems had to keep yanking me up while he rolled his eyes toward his friends. "Ya learn to skate at *Rush* or something?" he said. Rush was the name of the local school for mentally retarded kids. "No, but *you* did," I snap back before falling.

We sat and put the skates on. Only the mothers of the smallest babies stay in the chairs. I keep away from the babies. Don't need my heartstrings pulled that way. Lydia's father is out there on the pond, gliding across the ice on one long leg. Lydia too can skate like that. They do their father-daughter crazy eight kind of thing (he had a long black scarf flying behind him, and those wide-whale corduroy pants), then joining them are all the cousins, mothers, kids, Henry, and even the family bum, who skates, it seems to me, with great sarcasm, like his body is mocking the activity, at least initially. I stand by the edge and watch for a while. I watch how the family bum's body soon takes over; he can't help it, he's a good skater too, and now he is doing it with joy, it seems to me, the joy that comes with the body's great skill, where cynicism finally has no chance.

Lydia and Henry are holding hands.

The inevitable sight of it means more than it should, and my heart falls like a boulder into the endless space that is now my internal life. Couple-skating, right here in front of the family, it's like an announcement, it means everything, their stupid fate is sealed, the answer is yes, Henry is gloriously happy, the two of them are giggling and stopped over at the other side of the pond, and he's got his black-gloved hands on either side of her arms, and he's saying something, and she's shyly looking down, and now giggling, and yes, it's like a movie, they are stars and they have to kiss.

And then Henry looks around to find me, to see if I've seen this, to see how I'm taking it, because deep down, he knows. He knows my agony, but next to his happiness what can it mean? It's like having your health on a spring day when your friend has the flu. You can serve her some chicken soup, bring her flowers, but the blue sky, the birds, the light in the trees, that sense of possibility shining behind her heavy curtains, it makes you want to leave the room where she's aching, and you do, and you forget all about her.

I give him a little wave, a thumbs-up sign. His smile of gratitude is so real it's like a good-bye. What I mostly feel now is a scathing relief, since this has been coming at me like a train I always knew would flatten me. The flattening itself is strangely easier to take than the anticipation of it had been. My body is almost at peace. Something so restful about desolation.

Again I give him a thumbs-up sign, and the family bum

skates up to me and asks me if I'd like to get drunk after this little tradition is over.

I smile at him. "Drunk? Of course I'd like to get drunk. Smashed," I tell him. "Trashed. Shit-faced."

"Thatta girl."

He drives a Toyota with cassette tapes scattered all over the floor, dashboard, and backseat. He puts one of the tapes in, and I'm surprised to hear it's all Steve Martin, saying, *"Those French people have a different word for everything!"* The curious thing is, we drive in silence, not laughing at Steve Martin, but listening to his outrageous humor as if it's a grave political speech, or perhaps a eulogy.

"This is funny," I say.

"It is funny."

I think of my brother's friend, who never laughed, but always said, "That's funny." My brother called him the man who could recognize humor. I think to myself, It is Christmas Eve, and we are the people who can recognize humor.

"Maybe you should just take me home. You seem tired," I say.

He looks over at me. We're stopped at a red light. "I'm old," he says. "But I'm not a bit tired." He takes Steve Martin out and puts in some jazz. Coltrane, which cheers me, and assures me he's a man of taste.

"I'm just recovering from the evening on ice," he tells me. "I'll be fine after a while. I'm Cain, not Abel, okay? Call me *Unable.*"

I watch his profile as he concentrates on the road.

"That was a joke."

I tell him I thought it was funny.

He pulls into the lot of a liquor store, asks if I'd like to wait in the car or come in. I decide to wait. I decide I want time alone in the dark car to think about life. Then, as soon as he's gone, I decide I've had enough time alone in the dark car thinking about life, so I jump out and join him in the store.

"I thought rum would be good tonight. A good rum."

I smile. He looks so old under the lights. Out of nowhere I begin to think of him as Studs Terkel.

"Rum sounds good," I tell him.

"Is that coat warm?" he says.

"It's fine, Studs." It slips out. I could get hysterical laughing for no reason.

"Excuse me?"

"Nothing."

"You like rivers?"

"I like rivers."

"You like the Point?"

"Sure, Terkel."

"Studs Terkel," he says, putting two and two together. "I like the man. *The Good War.* But I don't know why, exactly, you're calling me by his name. Would you like to explain that, sister?"

"No," I say, and he throws his head back for a laugh.

We drive to the Point, the place in Pittsburgh where the three rivers meet.

On the way down to the river he asks me why I want to get drunk, what was I trying to forget, and I tell him. He nods, hardly saying a word, and I suspect I sound trite and pathetic.

"Subtle rewards will be yours," he says, mysteriously.

After that, we're quiet. We find a bench in the dark by the black river. He pours us rum and coke in yellow plastic cups.

"So tell me about yourself, Studs."

"Absolutely not. It's my least favorite subject."

I laugh, and he smiles over at me. For the first time, I see something in his face that looks like wisdom.

We watch a slow black barge push its way downstream.

"We could be quiet together all night like this. You ever been quiet with someone before?"

I laugh nervously and say I guess I haven't.

"Whatta ya think? Give it a shot?"

I shrug. A wave of loneliness comes over me. I don't want to be quiet. I want great talk. I want an old man's story, unraveling in my heart, distracting me, carrying me away.

But it's like he pulls silence down from the sky and covers us up. I feel suddenly that even if I wanted to speak, I couldn't. Or that if I did, the words would vanish in the air before their meaning could be felt. I'm afraid. I close my eyes and swallow down a sense of rising panic. Maybe he's crazy, this old wizard who pulled silence over the top of us like a see-through circus tent.

Maybe he'll throw me in the river, and then things will be even quieter.

No. This family bum exudes warmth. Settle down. Breathe.

I can hear the wind in the trees, the distant sound of traffic, the slap of the river against the bank, and his breathing, and my own breathing, and a sound like the moon's heartbeat. After a while passes I hear the rum pouring into a plastic cup, followed by coke. I take the cup and realize I would rather jump in the river myself than say "thank you" and tear the fabric of this silence.

Even my mind grows silent. Or nearly so. Maybe every so often Henry skates by, the sound of the blade sharp and disruptive. But out here by the river with this silence he seems infinitely smaller.

Maybe we're almost meditating.

We breathe, we look at the river, we breathe. The sky

opens up, gets bigger and brighter. We don't shift our posture. We don't fall asleep. In fact I feel radiantly awake.

A long time passes before he stands up. I stand up after him and then we walk back to the car. We listen to our footsteps crunching over half-frozen ground. He wears old brown boots.

In the car the silence is more intense, like we're indeed underwater, but still breathing magically, easily. He drives us to his apartment in a neighborhood called Swissvale, across from a little bowling alley. I once bowled there in high school with a boy named Sam Stein whose ambition was to be mayor. I remember how at the time it seemed incredible to me that Sam could imagine himself in such a position. My ambition at that time was to somehow survive high school.

On the old man's front porch the little bowling alley looks like a dream.

Upstairs he gets eight glasses and sets them on the table, then pours ice water into them from a jug. We each drink four, smiling now, understanding that neither of us will be the first to speak.

He shows me to a bed on what used to be called a sleeping porch. The kind of porch you find sometimes at the seashore, in the front of the house, with windows that swing open. In the corner of the sleeping porch is a card table, a deck of cards, and a little lamp. He plugs in a space heater. A statue of Mary is on the windowsill. My mother once had one like it.

He leaves me alone.

I sleep well, under a heavy red plaid quilt that smells like earth.

In the very early morning I hear him in the kitchen.

Will we talk? Will the family bum persona come back, the one I'd met just last night in the yard? And will I return too, with my voice shot full of yearning?

He turns and hands me coffee, cocks his head toward the door. Then I'm in my coat, following him down the steps and out into the cold so he can drive me home.

Before I get out of the car we grip each other's hands, and for a moment breathe in what feels like perfect unison.

The morning is cold, clear, a streak of red in the sky. The streak has a sound I could never describe.

For a moment I hesitate. I almost say, "Will you call me?" or "Can we be quiet again together sometime?" But I know, somehow, this is not to be repeated.

He lets go of my hands, smiles, and I stand and watch him drive away.

How lit with grace the world seems now—for these few moments by the curb where the sky shines red through the black arms of a bare tree, on a cold Christmas morning in Pittsburgh, Pennsylvania, in the year 2000.

What happened? What kind of magician was that family bum?

I get into bed. This life is big.

The Pastor's Brother

WERE YOU A THOUGHTFUL SORT seated with the pastor's brother at a long table of strangers one evening, he would likely draw your eye, though at sixty-two he was a man who liked to keep his profile low. The years of struggling to make a name for himself as a cabinetmaker were over. It was known that he was the best. He not only worked beautifully with wood, but carved intricate designs that recalled the meticulous beauty of other centuries.

He was soft-spoken, and his dark eyes were both kind and excessively vigilant. He was one-quarter Cherokee; it showed up in his bone structure, and years ago, in his night-black hair. He dressed in shades of brown or dark green, and had finally cut his ponytail in order to cultivate more privacy. The ponytail had invited too many people to approach him to ask whether he was Willy Nelson, or Willy Nelson's brother. In the old days he'd played along with this, made up stories about what Willy was like when he was a kid. "He and I would jump trains at night, back when America was more trains and fields than cars and lawyers."

The pastor's brother really had hopped into boxcars long ago, but was now relieved to live a life whose confines he knew well. Despite arthritis he worked with his wood, he taught cabinetmaking at the community college and woodworking at the local arts center, and had mentored young people for decades. He loved his wife, Rachel, and after twenty-six years of marriage was capable of believing that he was loved by her in return.

His daughter, Maria, lived in Oakland, California. She was an ex–drug addict apocalypse artist who sent him homemade cards revealing a streak of insane humor that scared him. She would feature President Bush dressed like a sexy waitress asking idiotic-looking customers in patriotic T-shirts, "How would you like your end-time sirloin cooked?" Everything was *end-time* with Maria. He tried not to think of her too often, but in his town a handful of minivans were adorned with bumper stickers that said *Warning*: *In case of rapture this vehicle will be unmanned.* That was a particularly annoying symbol of end-time wackiness, and wasn't Maria smart enough to know that end-time crap had existed since first-time? He knew the answer to that. She was smart enough, certainly, but something somewhere had gone wrong with her. "She came into the world with her screws loose, and that's how she'll leave it," his father had once remarked. His brother, the pastor, had defended her. "She's a good kid," he'd said. "We don't know the whole story. Give her time."

He loved his brother fiercely for those kinds of moments, despite all the Christianity, which he felt was an insult to their Cherokee grandfather, a figure who'd been inexplicably crucial to him as a child, a man who'd lived in a tiny house that had been flooded by the river's rising. He remembered himself as a small boy swimming through those ruined rooms, his grandfather's rocky laughter dancing in the water. The two of them sat together in a chair later that evening in a neighbor's house, listening to a ball game on the radio. How, he'd wondered later, could certain Christians in the wide, taut net of his family condemn a man who knew how to sit with a boy in a chair and listen to a ball game the very night his house gets flooded, the very night he loses the nothing he'd had? What kind of religion would exclude a man like him?

Back at the table of strangers, you'd also notice how the pastor's brother had dark eyes gently regarding whoever spoke to him; you'd see how generously he listened, nodding, smiling, making whoever talked with him feel utterly at ease. In fact, had he not been assertively male in appearance, he would've seemed almost womanly in this regard. He had none of the usual male discomfort in the face of talk; he didn't sit back and cross his arms over his chest, he didn't let his eyes wander around the room, nor did he interrupt, or ever try to dominate a conversation. He had such a deep sense of human vulnerability this listening was actually hard work; you could catch him wincing on occasion. These qualities, innate tendencies that had deepened thanks to a troubled daughter, made others value his presence and think of him as the salt of the earth.

One winter night when he was listening to NPR's account of the Muslims and Hindus killing each other in India, the pastor called.

They hadn't spoken since Christmas, and that had been a short, friendly talk, involving neither of their wives, who in past years had hung on downstairs phones trying to do a four-way chat, which the pastor's brother had always found excruciating. It wasn't just that he happened to be a born phone hater, the sort who gets lonelier and restless having to hear the disembodied human voice leaking out of a plastic receiver; it was that his wife, Rachel, on the other phone would laugh in a way that seemed reserved for the pastor alone. And something behind his breastbone would rise like hair on a cat's back, until he'd break in with "Why don't we talk one at a time," and they'd ignore him. He would then feel trapped by that familiar sense of isolation experienced most exquisitely when his brother and his wife addressed each other. His face burned with a humiliating jealousy; he would go and press his forehead against the window.

He was grateful that the calls lasted no more than twenty minutes or so. Then relieved when the pastor had grown so busy with his inner-city congregation years ago, more passionately committed than ever. The pastor and his wife, Claire, had almost no time to come visit after that. Claire was soft-spoken, a first-generation Latvian with warm blue eyes and an ability to quote long Latvian poems that seemed to always include wet brick streets. Quietly insightful, intelligent and somewhat melancholy by nature, she was an old friend by now, but too often during their visits, the pastor's brother would be *pretending* to talk to Claire, when really he'd be listening rapaciously to the conversation going on across the room, the ones where the pastor and Rachel would somehow fit Dietrich Bonhoeffer, John Coltrane, and Celtic myths into the same conversation. The ones that transformed his wife (beauty almost aggressively residing in her face as she listened), and to a lesser extent transformed the pastor too, though Claire and the rest of the world had never bothered to notice. He felt stranded during these times, and because in his heart he knew his daughter, Maria, lived her entire life feeling stranded, he'd turn to her in memory, aching for that little girl she'd been, crouched in the tree fort out back, curly-

haired with a tinge of wild light in her green eyes, her smiling lips a secret, her sandals and a worn blue dress she wore
like a uniform: The images seared. When he felt like that he'd
write her a letter so imbued with nostalgia he always ripped it
up a few hours later, despising its sentimentality. For all she
knew, he was a calm and ordinary father, often monosyllabic
on the telephone. Every so often sending her a check.

The pastor's call came just as he decided to turn the radio off.

"Tim?" The pastor's voice was like their father's: deep,
warm. Tim's own voice seemed by contrast thin, higher
pitched.

"Hey, John!"

"I've got news." Tim stood at the front door watching it
snow; his narrow street was wonderfully white in the lavender
light of evening. He still loved snow, after all these years. Still
loved the way it erased edges in the town's neglected streets.
Loved it in his wife's hair, in his dog's sleek black coat, in his own
hands when he packed it into a ball to throw. "What's up?" he
said, and imagined another grandchild had come into the
world. The pastor had five grandchildren already, all with bib-
lical names like Ruth and Noah, the oldest one a great violinist.

"I'm retiring."

"Retiring? You're kidding!"

"Hey, I'll be sixty-five."

"But you're—you're in the middle of things! You can't
retire! You're young!"

"I'm two months from sixty-five, brother."

Tim had broken out into a sweat; they would have to go to
Pittsburgh, they would go to the retirement party, they
would go stay in the old house, the one his wife loved, they
would stay for a week, and now Tim stepped outside onto the
front stoop and waved at a neighbor child, a fat little thing in

a blue coat and squeaky snow pants making tracks in the street. The child waved back, his face red and plump like an illustration, quaint like something Tim and his brother would have seen way back in the forties in Nebraska, where their mother had called them in from the lace-curtained kitchen window, long before John had blossomed into the spiritual man he was, long before he'd gone to Harvard Divinity School and made the entire family so proud they'd made Tim his shadow. Somebody had to be the shadow! They hadn't been emotionally sophisticated; in those days, who was? Tim hardly blamed them. In fact, he felt his own memories as clichés: Look at the brother, the pale one in the corner whose spark you can't see when the older brother is in the room. The older brother with his wide, freethinker mind (like his professor uncle) and his enormous heart (like his mother) and his quicksilver way of making everyone laugh with a one-liner. Tim was so serious, they thought, so burdened by his own jumbled thoughts and hopelessly inarticulate and emotional. (Beautiful music made him weep like a girl; he had learned to run and hide.) "A bit of the solipsist in that one," his uncle had once declared, but that was far from the truth; it was the world that interested Tim, and had there been a magic pill in those days to take the *self* out of his self, he'd have taken it more often than not. He often imagined that everything wrong with his daughter was a gnarled weed sprung from the soil of his own twisted genes.

Early in life, he'd become an expert at breaking commandments. Susan Harkins (famous in Twayne, Nebraska, for being half Jewish) became pregnant when the two of them were sixteen; they'd married. When the child was two months old they'd given him up for adoption to an older couple in town. (Through the years he'd tried unsuccessfully to track that son down, then given up.) Tim and Susan Harkins divorced after two years, when Tim was nineteen, and the

young ex-wife ran away with a vagabond, leaving Tim to settle into his role as black sheep. He'd had a yearlong affair
with Peg Cassidy, a petite married woman twice his age.
He'd stolen her husband's money and taken her away for a
week to Niagara Falls. He'd been arrested. His mother had
disowned him for a year and said he was a wild Indian like
his father's father, which he told her was a compliment.

But none of this memory could he take seriously; rather he
enjoyed superimposing his own face on the body of a black
sheep, then placing the sheep on a train. The sheep with his
own face would be framed in the window as the train slid out
of Nebraska into a sea of stars, Willie Nelson singing "This
Land Is Your Land," his Cherokee ancestors nurturing earth
in their graves.

"You could even drive," the pastor said. His voice was
beginning to fade. Was he on a cell phone? The pastor
wouldn't have a cell phone, would he? "It's not that far. If
Rachel still hates flying. . . ."

"Well, listen, I don't know about any travel, I mean after
September eleventh, Rachel is actually getting agoraphobic."
(The lie slipped out before he could stop it and now he was
ashamed.)

The pastor had indeed invited them for a week, was saying they'd be the guests of honor. Why did so many things
come true exactly the way you'd imagined? And why could
you still be such a fool at age sixty-two? He stood outside
with the phone now, letting the snow hit his face.

He said, "Hey, listen, John, we'll be there, we wouldn't
miss it for the world."

And heard the pastor sigh with gratitude. "You've always
been there, Tim," he said. "I hope Maria can come too,
though I'd understand if she couldn't. I'll just be glad to have
you beside me that day. I'm a little conflicted about this
retirement—"

"So don't do it!" Tim chimed in. "You're still young."

His brother laughed. "Not that conflicted. I'm ready, and Claire and I are excited about moving. Did I mention we're moving to New Mexico?"

"New Mexico!" Tim felt his face grow warm; he bent and scooped up some snow. Why did his brother have to retire to his wife's favorite place on earth? Such mean coincidence always made Tim believe in God.

". . . and there's a lot of Spanish-speaking people there so Claire and I are taking Spanish—have been all year."

"Great. Great. I'm really happy for you. It's just great."

"Yeah, well, thanks, Tim. I have to admit I get a little teary when I think about it all."

Tim was quiet. He didn't know what to say. Feelings charged out of his heart like wildebeest down a cliff. Feelings built of memories that showed up only in his dreams and were usually forgotten, but now, with clarity that kept him still, he saw John at fourteen with black hair against the hay in the barn where they'd wrestled, where he'd bitten John so hard he'd tasted blood.

And you didn't say a word about it. You were fifteen. You were down on the ground, looking up at me, shocked at having seen my rage. Under the shock was interest, and the beginning of compassion, since you were from the start a spectacularly evolved soul, brother John, and you'd already had your first religious experience by then, the one where you stood out in a field under the millions of Nebraska stars, and felt the pulse of the universe as the very voice of God saying in a language translatable only in that moment, "You are loved."

Did I ever tell you I had a very similar experience, only God said to me, in a language I could translate any moment of the day, "You are a loser"?

"Well, John," he said now, "I can understand getting teary. I mean, this has been your whole life."

"Yeah. It has, hasn't it."

A pause.

"So, Tim, you think Maria will come?"

"God knows."

"Yeah. I understand. So. How's everything going?"

"Fine. We're healthy. Busy. In fact, I should go, John. I need to get some firewood for tonight."

Tim had always spoken in shorthand to his brother about his own life. What was that urge to protect the details of his life from his brother's knowing? As if his brother could somehow take his life away from him just by knowing about it.

Rachel was thrilled. "I miss them! This will be wonderful. And I can give Claire that pot I made her, finally. Maybe even Maria will fly in for this."

"I'm glad you're excited. I don't feel like traveling."

They were in the car in the dark, on the way to the Hot Spot, where they'd get hot fudge sundaes and coffee and read the paper. It had stopped snowing. Rachel smelled like rose-petal lotion. She wore a bright scarf around her head. She was still, at fifty-six, too often the most beautiful creature he'd ever seen.

"You used to love to travel."

"But September eleventh. You said yourself—"

"I'm over it."

"That was quick."

She reached over and let her hand cup his kneecap. "Should I call Maria?" she said.

"I don't know." He drove with caution that made him feel elderly. Then he entertained a dark, familiar thought: that his whole life was a charade, that the deepest truth of his life would be revealed once again, in Pittsburgh, and that all this living as a good guy in upstate New York with his beloved wife and woodwork was like an exercise. The flimsiest, least challenged parts of himself could thrive here, and he could fool himself into thinking it was all right. That he had recovered himself. That he was solidly loved, and loving.

"I'll call Maria," he said.

"You will? Great." Maria had broken Rachel's heart long ago, in her earliest drug-addict days. It would never be healed. But Rachel had a lively, passionate mind that knew how to thrive like an indestructibly vibrant kite darting and rising above the darkest sea. Lately she had fallen in love (again) with Kierkegaard. She referred to him as Soren, like she might go have a cup of coffee with him if he wasn't dead. Tim envied her natural enthusiasm, and sometimes let himself be swept along in its current, such as last year when she became a bird fanatic. They'd gone to every marsh on the east coast. He'd spent five hundred bucks on binoculars. He'd wept seeing a blue heron up close.

He watched Rachel pack. "Do you need to pack so much?"

She looked at him. "What?"

"Nothing."

She laughed in the lamplight. She stepped up and kissed him, her silver earrings dangling. "This terrorism stuff is making you sweetly annoying. You're like an anxious pup at my heels. Why don't you go have a beer or something? Listen to Sonny Boy Williamson. He'll cheer you up. Or try calling Maria again! She's a whole different brand of terrorism."

He felt dismissed, stung by her anxious pup remark, but his dignity was a ship that sailed him wordlessly out of the room.

He did have a beer, and listened to Keith Jarret's haunting *Köln Concert*, so as not to be cheered up, and called his daughter. On her answering machine he left this message: "Hey there, it's your dad. Your uncle John would love to see you at his retirement party. I'll pay for the ticket if you want to come. Okay, let me know, and I'll—"

Maria picked up the phone. "Timothy?" She'd taken to calling him this fairly recently.

"That's me, kiddo," he said. He was impersonating a father now.

"I'd love to come see Uncle John's retirement party."

"You sound strange today."

She laughed. She dropped the phone, still laughing. Finally she was back. "I'm tripping my ass off."

He said nothing. He held the phone tightly. And then, from deep in his chest, a familiar sorrow rose in him that left him speechless. "Okay," he finally said. And he hung up.

He hadn't the heart to tell Rachel about the call when she hauled out the bulging plaid suitcase, frayed from so many years of use.

"I'm excited!" she said.

When a child knocked on their door selling candy for school, Tim went with her to see the child; he liked when random kids appeared at the door. This little girl was unsmiling and homely. "Would you like to buy a candy bar to help support East Hills school?" she said in a monotone. Her nose was running. Tim wanted to pull her into the house, wanted to sit her down and discover how she endured her life. "Aren't you cold out here?" he said. "No," mumbled the girl, and her blue eyes darted to the side. The sleeves of her coat were too short and he saw the impossible fragility of her bluish wrists.

"Are you sure? It feels cold to me."

She shook her head.

"If you were cold, you could come in a while and have something warm to drink by the fire."

The girl looked frightened now. *What kind of world do you think this is, mister?*

"I know, I know, you need to move on to the next house and make some money." He took a ten-dollar bill from his pocket. "Here. Give me a candy bar."

The girl handed him one, and began rifling through a stack of ones. "You get nine dollars change."

"Keep it."

A sly smile came to her lips, and she looked down. "Thanks." She turned and walked away.

Rachel shut the door and looked at him. "You liked her."

"I liked her."

"I like that you liked her."

She smiled at him, an old desire flashing in her eyes, and kissed him on the mouth.

"I reached Maria," he said, and Rachel stiffened and stepped back.

"And?"

He hesitated, torn between wanting to tear her excitement to shreds and wanting to protect her heart, always.

"She's not coming. Too busy."

"How did she sound?"

"Fine. Not a word about the end-time."

In the airport that morning it was initially a relief for Tim to see his brother looking old, and then sadness set in. John looked vulnerable, the broad forehead lined and the eyes sunken just a bit. In Tim's memory his brother always appeared in his prime. Seeing the inevitable age softened Tim, as it had before, and now the good will inside of his fear woke, his heart leapt forward, he embraced John and said, "It's good to see you." Rachel and Claire talked all the way out of the airport. Tim saw how Rachel had hardly looked at John. *So much was his own sick creation*. Wasn't it and hadn't it always been? He walked beside his brother in the

Pittsburgh airport and felt invigorated by the intensity and purity of his admiration. My brother, this man of integrity. He might be a Christian, but he's decent about it, and deep, and he's not a bigot.

Now they were sharing an old joke—its roots going all the way back to 1949—"I like your Binky Leanard shoes," John said, and Tim broke out into laughter.

Behind them Rachel said, "God I love to see those two together!"

The first part of the retirement party was held in an old renovated theater, a charming old place where Gene Kelly had once danced. It sat across from the church in one of the city's poorest neighborhoods. The pastor, with the help and support of his wife, had been at the helm of transforming the church; before they'd come it was a dying monolith serving mostly white, upper-middle-class people who drove in from the suburbs. Now the mammoth cathedral was ecumenical and alive with the full human spectrum.

This Pittsburgh church was so much more complex and of the world than his previous church—the tame Midwestern one that Tim privately mocked for being just that. Even Rachel had said the last church was too lily white for her tastes, and Tim was glad, since he liked anything in those days that protected him from imagining Rachel was in love with his brother. Even after the two of them—John and Rachel—had once stayed up all night talking, at least the next day driving home Rachel had said, "I was starting to go crazy there. It was just a little too clean-cut."

"Yeah, well, that's John," Tim had said. Which was ridiculous. That wasn't John at all.

This was more John. This place, this old theater where now they sat in the dark with over a hundred strangers and nieces and nephews and a handful of people they knew as John's friends, waiting for the retirement show to begin. John and Claire were seated up in the balcony; an old woman from the congregation had wanted to feed them pastries and champagne and had set up a little table there.

An old Beatles song began to play. "There are places I remember, all my life, though some have changed." Rachel squeezed his arm. The slide show started. John as a baby, there in the backyard, sunlit, a curl on top of his head, and Rachel's hand flew up to cover her mouth. "Look at him," she whispered, and her head bent to the side as if to get every possible angle. But the slide had already been replaced with John at age six, this one formal: his hair slicked down, little body in a suit, his smile radiant and his eyes already shining with purpose. "This kind of thing kills me," Rachel said.

This surprised him. She was not a sentimental woman. He imagined she would resist this display were it not all about John.

And the Beatles played on, and now a shot of the lanky brothers, age nine or ten, their arms around each other, a horse behind them that Tim remembered had belonged to a fat blind man down the road. Rachel squealed at this one and squeezed Tim's hand. "Look at you, Tim!" But the picture for Tim evoked something close to nausea. (He had never forgiven himself for being that child, had never known forgiveness was necessary; because he'd for so long mocked himself in memory, he closed his eyes now, was relieved when the next slide came up and erased him.) Glad now to see the childhood part of the show was closing, and to look at John in high school, the valedictorian, of course, who back then had been able to include Jesus in his speech, the guy who all the girls loved but who'd been too busy reading his Calvin and Augustine and Saint John of the Cross, and besides he wanted to lose his virginity to whoever his wife would be, even though waiting was too much torture and he actually ended up all too humanly and admirably losing it in a car with Rita Pers, a shapely atheist transplant with a Brooklyn accent whose favorite expression was "Oh, come on, John, spare me!"

"But of all these friends and lovers . . ." (Rachel was singing along for a moment.)

The audience murmured and laughed at the slides, sometimes breaking into applause. They watched their pastor captured in Divinity School, his idealism shining in his young face; they watched him get engaged and grow sideburns in the seventies to go with his plaid seventies clothes (this got a good laugh), and they watched him marry Claire, who supported her husband with a love so deep you could feel it running between the two of them like a river, said one of the young women church members, and then Simon and Garfunkel were singing "Time it was and what a time it was. . . . " Tim loved that old song; he'd been almost young when he got the record, when he and his friend Saul had lived that year on Chiming Avenue in the blue dilapidated house with the huge tomatoes out front. Saul the poet. Saul who was impossibly dead. Had been dead since he was fifty-eight and jogging his heart out by the Atlantic Ocean two days after he'd married for a second time.

Tim came back to the slides, where John was a young father with a son on his shoulders. He became aware that Rachel was teary-eyed. She held his hand, and now they were showing a video where members of the congregation spoke about John. (The man who introduced the video was flagrantly, joyfully, stereotypically gay, and explained that they'd had to edit the video so as not to embarrass the pastor; apparently certain members had gone overboard in their assessment of him. Especially the women, he added, and everyone laughed easily; the pastor could flirt the way only the truly well-behaved can flirt, the depths of his basic decency putting everyone at ease.)

Tim watched Rachel carefully now; he saw the smile of recognition. *Especially the women.*

He missed Maria fiercely, suddenly. He wanted to get up from his seat and find a pay phone. *Anything, anything you need. I'm here for you.* Then remembered her hollow laughter. *I'm tripping my ass off.*

On the video they'd interviewed John's three children. Tim especially loved his younger nephew, Peter, who'd spent half the summer with him the year he'd turned fourteen. An awkward kid who had never held a hammer, he'd allowed Tim to teach him fundamentals of the shop, and after a month or so confided in Tim that he was in love with a girl and it was just *killing* him. The two had gone hiking that evening for three hours, Tim determined to show the boy how waterfalls and ancient birch trees and bats under a far-flung moon could offer the heart a little reprieve.

This nephew, nineteen now on the video, looking confident and adult in his black leather jacket, said he'd asked his father if there was anything big he felt he still had to accomplish. The answer was no.

No. The answer spoke of a peace that was beyond the realm of Tim's imagination. To experience that degree of satisfaction. His brother had set out to live a certain kind of life, and he'd done just that. He'd thrown himself into it, worked *tirelessly* for forty years, and while he'd had his hard times, and bouts of depression, a net of faith had kept him on his path. A life that wasn't wayward. How many in this world would ever get to sit back and feel the stubborn coherence of their own story this way?

"A beautiful life," Rachel whispered. "That's what this is."

A flame rose in Tim. "And you're wishing you were Claire."

She only laughed. "God no. I couldn't handle it."

What did that mean?

And why had she taken what he'd said in stride?

Why hadn't she turned in her seat and said, "What the hell is that all about, Tim? What do you mean I'm wishing I was Claire?"

And now the motley church choir did a few gospel tunes—maybe these were John's favorites. And then they were calling John and Claire up onto the stage, and people stood and clapped and clapped, and both John and Claire were able to thank everyone with extraordinary graciousness. John said he imagined after they'd all seen his seventies wardrobe they might be reconsidering their opinions of him. Everyone laughed.

"I'd like to introduce you all to some special people," John said now, and called up his children, his old friends Michael and Anita Nells (who looked like Sophia Loren), and the Burnhams, and Claire's sister Louise the dog trainer, cousin Richard from Alabama, and finally, Tim and Rachel. They rose and walked to the stage, and John ushered them over right next to him, and Tim found himself slinging his arm around his brother, his palms wet and his eyes suddenly stinging with tears under the stage lights as everyone clapped. This should not be such a complicated moment, he thought, shamed, proud, wanting to embrace his brother, wanting the two of them to be alone together, boys in a field after a whole day of running wild in the dry land of sticks and stones and old Nebraska sky, wanting to look into his brother's face and say "I love you can you help me." And wanting to invite Rachel to go visit another galaxy. But here she was, kissing John right on the lips.

"I love you, John!" she said.

"And I love you, Rachel."

And Tim felt like his own camera, capturing this moment

that he'd turn over in his mind later, developing it until it was sharp, punishing. And he embraced Claire and shook hands with their friends and joked with his nephews and now it was time to cross the street in the rain of early evening and eat a meal in the basement of the Cathedral of Hope and he felt crazy and loose and responsible for Maria three thousand miles away and probably coming down from her trip in a filthy end-time apartment.

Shrimp, steak, fresh vegetables, big salad. This church, which under John had tripled its sizable endowment, had gone all out to say its good-bye in style. Nothing like John's other church, where it had always been churchified meat loaf and string beans. Beside the table where John and Claire and their kids sat, Rachel and Tim sat at a table with some young people, married couples whose children were upstairs being baby-sat, and a gay man and his partner who had recently adopted a five-year-old foster child, a boy whose picture they passed around. They all had guessed that Tim was John's brother. They were grateful for his presence at the table and only wanted to tell him how much they adored their pastor. How he had changed their feelings about religion. How he was the most compassionate and open-minded person they'd ever encountered other than Mr. Rogers. How the pastor had married the gay couple. One black-eyed woman with a Boston accent spoke to Tim with a strange, confidential urgency. "Your brother knows how to *receive* love. It's not just that he can give it. What impresses me is the way he can *receive* it. My own father, he couldn't take it. Nobody in my family could take it. You'd give them a hug and they'd die from embarrassment! If you ever said I love you to any of them they'd have to be rushed to the emergency room! But your brother, I swear, when I hug him, he can *take* it." She began to tear up, and Tim reached to pat her hand. She kept her eyes downcast. She said she didn't know why he had to move away. Then she stood up, excused herself, and took off for the ladies' room, up the steps. Tim watched her exit, lingering over her words. He thought of following her. He thought of his daughter. He wondered if he'd known how to receive love. The taller of the gay men was saying how his foster son had first been abandoned in a Kings Family restaurant when he was two.

Tim asked to see the picture of the boy again, and the child's face drilled a hole in his heart that filled for a moment with stabbing light.

"He looks like a great kid."

"We're very lucky."

He wanted to be home. He wanted to work with some old oak. Wanted to walk the dog, to see a friend, to find the relative peace of the quotidian, who cares if it was partly a lie. He wanted to be home.

He feared these days of terrorism; it was true. They would not get to hear John's last sermon, but he'd make sure they got a copy of it. They'd hit the road tomorrow afternoon, or the next. Everyone would understand. Everyone was afraid, deep down.

On the way back to the house he told Rachel he wanted to leave the next day. He told her he was exhausted, he might be getting sick, and he feared the world.

"You fear the world?" she said, a smile in her tone.

"Anthrax. Bombs. Chemicals."

"They say you have a better chance of getting struck by lightning than coming into contact with anthrax."

"I know three people who got struck by lightning," he said.

"Who?"

"Two kids—those young lovers kissing on the beach in Wildwood, New Jersey, back the year Maria was born. And Bernard Lynch's mother."

"You didn't know those kids, Tim."

"What difference does it make? We were in Wildwood then. We might have been swimming in the ocean with them the day before they fried together."

"What exactly are we talking about?"

"Dying."

"So you want to leave tomorrow?"

"Or the next day. Maybe that would be more decent. I remember Bernard Lynch's mother played a *mean* ukulele."

She reached out and touched the hand that was not on the wheel. "You're getting really strange in your old age, Tim."

"You know I'll take that as a compliment, so why say it?"

She was quiet.

He parked in front of the house John and Claire stayed in; it was owned by the church, it was stone, and big with character, a garden of roses in the summertime out back, and a huge sycamore in front that now stood bare and groping into the dark.

"What are you thinking, Rachel?" he said now, turning off the motor.

"I don't know."

He looked at her. "Are you angry with me?"

"No. I don't know."

"What?"

"Maybe you should tell me."

"Tell you what?"

She sighed. "Let's just go in."

"No."

"No?"

He nearly broke. He nearly confessed a lifetime of his

deepest pain. He was so close to doing it his heart pounded in his chest. *Tell me how it burdens you, in those secret chambers of your heart, tell me how you wish you were spending your life with my brother. It will be such a relief! You'd have a different child then, too, and a great violinist grandson, your heart might even be whole.*

But he only looked at her in the car, and seeing her beautiful dark eyes wounded by confusion, he felt the weight of their long years together, took a breath and said, "I mean yes, I'm sorry, let's go in now. Let's just go in."

Maybe he was tired of the tight leash he'd held around his own neck for so many years of visits.

Maybe he was tired of the tightrope he danced upon and only wanted to watch himself fall and fall, straight into a whole different kind of life where he could see his decency in shreds. Where he could see his pain in shards. Where he could join his daughter in a chaos that defied description.

Maybe it was the three big glasses of Merlot.

Really it didn't matter what the reason was.

Rachel threw her head back because the pastor was telling a funny story. She grabbed onto the pastor's forearms. The room began to spin. Tim called over from the couch where he sat next to his nineteen-year-old nephew, "John, Rachel, why not go on upstairs for a good fuck and get it over with?"

A heavy silence fell, thick with everyone's disbelief. Nobody moved.

Then the nephew beside Tim bent in half, spit out his ice, and burst into nervous laughter punctuated by "Holy shit!" Everyone seemed to be looking at the white ice on the red carpet for a moment. Then the nephew got up off the couch and walked into the kitchen, dragging his sister, who'd stood shocked in the doorway, along with him. On the other side of the room Claire put down her drink, closed her eyes, and turned toward her sister. "Did that just happen?"

As for Rachel, she was a statue, standing beside the statue pastor. Tim felt he had torn the roof off the house. Had torn the skin off his body. And yet for a second he felt violently happy. The pastor was so white-faced, he looked ill.

"Uh, Tim, can we go outside for a moment?"

Rachel bent down beside Tim now. "What the hell was that?" she whispered. "Are you out of your mind?"

"Yes."

The pastor came and took him by the hand.

Tim thought they were strange old boys moving quickly out of the house and into the March darkness.

They went and stood by the tree.

"I can explain," Tim said.

"No, no. You don't have to."

"I don't?"

"No, you don't. Unless you want to."

"No. I'm sorry. I'm sorry."

"Okay. I think I know that."

Silence.

"We could climb this tree if we weren't such geezers," the pastor said.

And Tim pulled himself up on the lower branch, swung his body over so that he was riding the branch like a horse, his long legs dangling down on either side. "When Maria was small she wanted to *be* a tree. That's what she answered when they asked her what she wanted to be when she grew up."

"I remember you telling me that. Come on down, Tim. You're nuts."

"I am. I really am. I got you beat on that one, Johnny. I'm truly out of my mind, aren't I?"

"I don't see it that way, Tim. I just want you to come down."

Now Tim was climbing up to the next highest branch.

"That's enough, Tim, no higher," said the pastor.

But there was no stopping him. He was going all the way up. It wasn't even that difficult. In spite of his trembling, his body filled with a desperate agility. When he finally reached the near top, up there in the black sky, in certain danger of falling to his death, a great, shocking compassion for himself swept through him, the sort he'd only felt for other people before this moment.

He looked down at John and thought, weeping, I know who I am now! I'm an old man up in a tree, getting ready to tell my lovely loveliest of loving brothers the story of my life.

GUIDING LIGHT

I WAS TWELVE WHEN A WOMAN NAMED ANNE moved into the apartment across the hall from us. My mother and I let her settle in for a week before we walked to her door with a pound cake and welcomed her to the building, though I thought an extension of sympathy may have been more appropriate, considering what surrounded her. The building itself wasn't so bad—typical brick five-story apartment house across from a playground in Pittsburgh. But the tenants, ourselves included, were unpredictable. Our landlord was a hippie named Bert who had inherited millions from his father; Bert didn't mind problem tenants. He didn't even evict Olive Sibley, an old woman on the first floor who had birds, wild and domestic, careening around the empty rooms of her apartment, the windows open in case they cared to leave, which it seemed they didn't. Olive Sibley with her wild white hair in the lobby by the mailboxes grasping your hand and whispering her name in a confidential tone that implied a world of outsiders who'd never be privileged to hear it. Sometimes you would see Olive sitting sidesaddle on the ledge of her open window, waving like a woman on a ship moving away from land. Other times she looked furious, alone in her black coat by the fence at the playground, cursing under her breath. When kids made fun of her, my mother scolded them. "She's a human being!" she'd yell.

On the third floor lived another human being, the widower Irving Rooch, and his new wife, Natasha, and the four blond, feral Rooch boys, who went barefoot into November. Irving Rooch was friendly, and worked hard in a bar, but once he tried to saw the doors off his Chrysler in the middle of the night. My mother had yelled down, "Hey, what's going on down there?"

Irving Rooch had yelled back, "I'm tryin' to saw the doors off my car!"

Telling the story the next morning to my father, my mother ended with, "Poor Irv's had a hard life." It was her highest compliment, I see now.

I didn't like the place when I was twelve, I wanted something else, something like Alicia Montgomery's duplex on Darlington Street with its enormous, spotless kitchen, and the father reading *National Geographic* and talking about the habitat of prairie dogs at the dinner table, and the mother brushing your hair at her marble vanity, then taking you to the Carnegie art museum on Saturdays. "So I have a daughter who likes going to *museums*?" my mother said, in strange wonder, when I told her about my time with the Montgomerys.

Now that I'm a grown woman living amid the busily employed, who duck in and out of apartments as if the air itself is to be avoided, I'd welcome back Olive and Irving. Or Anne, I'd welcome Anne, though she was much quieter. The day we gave her the pound cake she smiled thoughtfully in her doorway, her dark blue eyes looking first at my mother, then at me. Then she spoke: "How nice. Come on in."

I was already intrigued by this woman with the silver-streaked hair who seemed clothed in silence. Her place appealed to me because I was a container of chaos and the rooms were stark with definition, taming a few layers of that chaos as I drank them in. She had a white baby grand piano in one room. Nothing else but a corner table with a vase of wildflowers. We followed her into the kitchen that smelled of oil paints. Covered canvases lined up against one wall. A painting of a pair of old boots kicked into the sky hung on another wall.

Anne wasn't chattering. I was used to chattering women. Was she angry or just odd? She asked us to sit and have tea, so we did, though my mother was strictly a coffee person; she was twenty-eight and had four kids; coffee got her through.

The kitchen brimmed with sunshine that seemed not to belong to Pittsburgh. It was French sunshine, I felt. Or English. Sunshine I'd seen only on *Children's Film Festival* on rainy Sunday afternoons. I imagined a history for Anne that involved a village, herself a child walking down cobblestone streets with Skinny and Fatty, the kids from one of those imported films.

Anne cut the pound cake, facing the window. Her dark hair was pulled back with a red rubber band. She poured tea into thick cups, the sort you'd find in an old luncheonette. Nobody spoke; she poured, we watched.

"So, are you originally from Pittsburgh?" my mother finally said—always her first question.

"Oh no. I grew up in the west until I was fourteen, then moved to New Jersey." Anne looked at my mother, and then at me. We stared at each other quite openly, until I grew shy and looked away.

"I can't imagine," my mother said, as if Anne had explained she'd come from the moon.

"So you've been here all your life?" Anne said.

"All my life."

"That must be something. That connection you must feel to this place."

My mother said, "Uh-huh."

"I don't think I can even imagine what it would be to have that sense of home," Anne said. She made it sound like a compliment and my mother took it that way.

"Well thanks. I just can't imagine not living here where I grew up," she said. "My sisters, my cousins, we all stayed."

"It's beautiful, I think," Anne said.

My mother smiled. "So you're a painter and a piano player."

Anne was looking at my hands now. She wasn't answering. My mother finally said again, "A painter and a piano player."

"Yes, yes. Look at those hands! Those hands should play the piano."

We all looked at my hands on the solid wooden table. For a moment they seemed to glow from within.

My mother held up her own hands. "And look at mine! Dishpan hands! These hands should go wash the dishes!" She began to gulp down the rest of her tea.

Anne watched her, a bit puzzled, and I blushed, embarrassed for my mother, wishing for a moment that she was not connected to me, fearing that Anne would judge me for it. My mother was not an educated woman. She had graduated early from high school at sixteen to marry my father. She read fat romance novels. She had never been to a museum, and the art she hung was made of yarn, or those paintings of girls with the big heads and enormous black eyes set low in their faces. At twelve I was beginning to develop a snobbery I didn't understand.

"I just love music," my mother was saying as she rose from the table. "Do you play any Burt Bacharach?"

"Oh, sure, I could," Anne said, and when her eyes flashed

over to me, for a moment I was fearful that she was mocking my mother.

"I just love his stuff," my mother said and sighed, and took her teacup to the sink. "So, welcome!" she said, and then we were leaving.

Back in our own kitchen my mother said, "Another odd duck for the building, huh?"

I shrugged.

"She's nice, though, huh?"

"Yep."

Later I heard my mother tell her friend Lorine on the phone, "We got a new neighbor. A mixture of a nun and an artsy-fartsy."

Nun because she wore no blue eye shadow, no lipstick, no bleach in her hair, no nail polish, I supposed, like my mother and Lorine. And she had that quiet about her whose source was surely the luxury of her own reflections. Not that the nuns who taught me had any of that.

"So do you want to take piano lessons?" Anne said. It was fall, I was in my school uniform bouncing a ball on the sidewalk. Though it was warm, Anne was in a coat that looked like an Olive Sibley coat, and for a moment I took my affection back. I didn't want her to be too strange. I wanted her to walk that thin line between strange and ordinary, or to be ordinary and secretly wonderful. Why was she in that winter coat? And why did her eyes look so urgent?

"I don't think my mom would let me," I said. "Too much money."

"I'd give them for free, if you'd let me paint you."

"Paint me? You want to paint me?"

"You'd make a great subject, I think."

"I'll have to ask my mom."

"Of course. Just let me know." She smiled, and I felt again my rush of curious affection for her. I watched her walk away, her dark silver-streaked braid hanging down her back, swinging with her sturdy stride.

Later I jumped up and down in our kitchen with my hands folded into prayer. "Please oh please can I ma can I ma?"

My mother just looked at me. Maybe she was envying my energy.

"She said I'd make a great subject!" I whined.

Lorine was at the table watching this display; my mother had set Lorine's hair, as she did every Thursday, and now a net covered her pink foam curlers. Her husband, a man I'd grown up calling Uncle Lou, had moved the year before to Chicago with a twenty-two-year-old girl, leaving Lorine with Lou Junior and Mary Pat, thin, pale, long-fingered children whose claim to fame was that neither of them had ever sneezed. Lorine would sit with them when they had colds and coach them. "A-chhooo!" she'd say, and the confused children would repeat the word.

"I don't know. What do you think, Lorine? Should I let her take piano from the woman across the hall?"

"I'd beware," Lorine said, eyebrows raised so the whole head of curlers lifted a bit. I could always count on not being able to count on Lorine.

"She is a little different," my mother said.

"Isn't everyone a little different?" I argued. They ignored me. Mary Pat and Lou Junior were pushing matchboxes on the floor with my little brothers, using my feet as hills.

"You kids go get lost, get out of here, scram," Lorine told them, and they ignored her, as usual.

"Please, I really want to play piano! I'll learn how to play 'This Guy's in Love' and 'Knock Three Times' and 'I Beg Your Pardon.'"

My mother looked down at me with those pale green eyes weighted with what I can recognize now as the deep fatigue that ruled her young life. "I guess you can give it a try," she said.

Lorine sighed. "You spoil her, Shirley. The kid gets whatever she wants."

Lorine was one of those women with so many regrets she couldn't stand looking at any version of the girl she had once been, a girl who still had choices. I didn't understand that then; I thought she hated me for mysterious reasons, or because I refused to pull my shoulders back when she reminded me I had crummy posture and would end up with scoliosis. But Lorine was staying for dinner; sloppy joes, her favorite, my mother tossing the meat with a wooden spoon, radio playing. My father would sit in a bar down on the South Side until eight or so; Lorine and my mother would sit in the kitchen and drink cheap wine called Night Train, and I'd be expected to come to the aid of the little kids, should a crisis arise. That night I accepted my role gladly, spinning the kids around in circles in the playground across the street, daydreaming about my new life with Anne the artist, my eyes on the moon and the big black sky.

After my first few lessons with that elegant woman (she wore delicate wire-frame glasses when she taught and afterward fed me expensive chocolates and good coffee—my first cup), I began practicing piano at my school in a large empty gym, with the lights off. Down the hall was the brightly lit pool where girls my age swam; I could hear the echo of their laughter and shrieks, imagine their long legs kicking underwater or shivering purple by the poolside while Sister Thomas Aquinas, in full habit, paced with her whistle by the pool's edge. The thick smell of chlorine wafted down the hall;

I remembered it stinging my eyes and turning my hair green the year before. This year I couldn't take all that locker-room nakedness, the peeling off of wet suits, the goose bumps and gawkiness, the dread that my own body was horribly abnormal in some way. I'd grown four inches in a year. My best friend had moved. I was determined not to replace her with some new sidekick. Her absence served as a presence. I played the piano picturing her buried under the leaves of Ohio. Her new school, she had written, was a *hell-hole full of morons*. She had included unflattering cartoon versions of everyone she'd met, all of them drooling, or cross-eyed and saying, "Duh, what's my name?"

I'd fool around on the keys for hours, until the streetlights poured in through the high barred windows and told me it was dark outside. The wet-haired girls from the pool would parade by the open doors of the gym, laughing and talking, having no idea I was there behind the piano in the dark.

Still, Anne was not impressed with my musical ability. I didn't have a very fine sense of rhythm, and I was really only interested in learning pop songs, sad songs like "Fire and Rain," and finally Anne gave up on teaching me scales. But she was excited with me as someone to paint.

The first time she painted me I had to wear an old red dress that smelled faintly of vinegar. It had a lace collar that had yellowed. I thought it was a terrible dress, but it wasn't uncomfortable. I sat there on a simple blue chair and watched her eyes peer and squint at me, watched her face take me in with concentration I'd never seen before. I felt such acute self-consciousness of my own body as an object in that red vinegar dress I almost got up and ran around the room in an attempt to shake myself back into myself. But something always shifted; I relaxed under her mysterious gaze. I was freed, perhaps because the world of conventional judgments felt far away in that place. I was made of shapes, and color.

In that first small painting I was a cross between myself and an Edvard Munch girl with all kinds of furniture sliding toward me, a window behind my head where a tiny brass lamp floated in the pink, surrealist sky. "Now don't look at this painting as if it's a mirror," Anne assured me. "I'm not a realist." My knees were bony as an old woman's, I thought, terrible looking, and my shoulders were full of tension, and my neck too long and pale. She had rendered the buds I had for breasts accurately, I thought, embarrassed. But she had given me such beautiful eyes. Much better than my real eyes. So luminous, with such depth, the more I looked at them the more I was able to see how insignificant the bony knees were.

It took at least a month of sitting for this one painting, and near the end my mother knocked on Anne's door, then stormed in before Anne could answer, my youngest brother asleep on her shoulder.

"At least show me the painting!" she said. I hadn't noticed anything brewing in her; in fact, I hadn't noticed her at all lately. I watched her now with shame; she was in a housecoat, her hair full of silver clips, her white calves fat, I suddenly saw with a pang. My brother's undershirt looked gray.

My mother stood and looked at the painting, while Anne, her concentration broken, went to the kitchen in her black smock, saying, "I'll make us some tea," her voice soft with defeat.

"That doesn't look a thing like you!" my mother whispered, smiling, relieved, it seemed to me.

"She's not even a realist!" I whispered back.

"But you look like a mental patient!" she said, her voice rising, lips compressed to hold in laughter.

"You don't understand! Just be quiet!"

Anne called us for tea; the orderly kitchen was like another painting we could step into. A smooth black rock sat on the sill over the sink. The sky pressing its blueness up against the screen like it wanted in. The grains of the wood in the table, swirling.

"So Gracie tells me you're not a realist," my mother said, smiling.

"Right," Anne said. She seemed a bit baffled, as if she'd just come away from a long, solitary swim.

"Why do you need Grace to sit for you then?" my mother said. Anne looked down into her tea and said she was using me as a starting place. That she worked with planes and angles and ideas. Combinations of things.

We sat and drank our tea in uncomfortable silence that was broken by my brother waking up in tears. "What's wrong, little boy? You got a fever? We'll leave these two alone now," my mother said, getting up.

"Don't forget where you live," she added.

She rushed out.

"Maybe you're spending too much time here," Anne said.

"No, no, no," I said. "I don't think so. Really."

So we went back to work.

Back to the shifting perceptions of my own body in the chair, back to Anne's blue eyes behind her glasses, her bare feet or worn moccasins, the sunlight or gray light in the room. I remember her serving ginger snaps on a red plate one afternoon, and being startled because they were so mundane, unlike her usual offerings. I remember she played the song "Standing in the Shadows of Love" on her record player once, and that I imagined the song made her remember an old love, a man who had died young in Paris. She asked me all sorts of questions about school, and my lost Ohio friend, and I answered them happily in great detail, amazed at how interesting I could sound in the presence of her genuine curiosity.

It was a little more than a year, this kinship, and my mother hated it, and I didn't care. I felt that year like my mother was a box I was clawing my way out of. When my mother and Lorine watched *Guiding Light* on summer afternoons, too alert on percolated coffee, they'd wait for commercials to tease me as I walked through the living room.

"So what are you doing with the rest of your day? Let me guess. You're gonna go sit on your ass across the hall for another painting they can hang up in Western Psych!"

"Whatever you say, ladies."

"At least get some fresh air once in a while."

"Maybe I'll avoid fresh air and normal things for the rest of my life."

"She's gonna turn out like Francie Bartusiak!" Lorine yelped, and the two of them laughed, and I bit my tongue so I wouldn't ask who Francie Bartusiak was.

"You two can be so revolting," I mumbled, but the power of the real disgust I felt alarmed me.

I had sudden moments when I missed my mother, whoever she had been.

"Hon, we're just jaggin' you," my mother assured me.

But I knew she was angry and hurt that I'd pulled away. I'd always been her girl. My father wasn't around much—a man of his time, he worked and he went to the bar and he slept, and if he didn't sleep he read the paper, and you better not disturb. He wasn't a bad man, just tired, so tired all the time. He had a way of squinting at the mess in our apartment as if he'd never seen it before, as if it were completely baffling to him. "I need to get out of here," he'd say to the air, and then he would, he'd get out of there.

So I had been my mother's confidante, the one who watched late-night movies with her in her bed with bowls of rice pudding, the one who she took shopping downtown with her when she bought a new dress, valuing my opinion over anyone's, even Lorine's. I was the one who gave her back rubs at the end of the day, her deepest pleasure, no doubt.

And now I wanted nothing to do with her. I would not get near her; I was afraid she was contagious. Sometimes she would come into my bedroom late at night, sit on the edge of my bed, and watch me sleep, though I was only pretending to sleep, and my whole body was clenched in anger, feeling her presence as a terrible invasion of my privacy, my body, while I prayed for her to disappear.

One day I had taken a bus to the South Side with Albie Rooch, the middle of the blond Rooch brothers. I had admired Albie from afar for years, had entertained all kinds of fantasies about him, and now, here he was, an eighth-grader, walking beside me on train tracks, his usually bare feet in faded black high-top sneakers. Trees made sparkling green walls on either side of us. Albie wore a muscle shirt and cutoff jeans and was talking in his long-winded way about the war mongrels who ran the world, and I was agreeing with everything he said, nodding encouragingly, like a girl.

That's when I saw Anne and another woman walking toward us. They seemed so out of place I thought I must be imagining it. The other woman I'd seen twice before, in Anne's apartment, but I'd forgotten her name.

"Hey," Albie Rooch said. "There's the lezzy."

"That's Anne," I argued. "Don't say that."

"You don't know she's a lez?"

Now Anne and her friend were approaching us.

"Hi, Anne!" I said, my heart pounding.

"Hi," Anne said, smiling. "Remember Margie? Margie, this is Grace and this is . . ."

"Albie," I said, and he was looking off into the sky, arrogant, disdainful, and bored.

Anne said something benign about the beauty of the day, and I looked at her with new, suspicious eyes, and saw that

Albie was right, and it hit me all at once, in the stomach. No man in her life, no makeup, this friend with the haircut like a man's. How had I not seen it all before?

"Not much to say today, Gracie?" Anne said, because I looked down at my feet, hating that I hadn't known, hating that I'd associated myself with her, that she'd meant so much to me, that she'd done all those paintings of me.

"No, not much to say," I said, too loudly, and off I ran with Albie, down the tracks. We wandered up into the trees, where he got a hungry kiss, as if kissing him that way could somehow obliterate whatever I felt for Anne.

"So you finally got tired of Anne, I see," my mother said one August night. The little kids were in bed, Lorine was in Sea Isle City with her kids visiting her sister, and my mother and I were up late watching *Marcus Welby, M.D.*

"Yep," I said.

It was dark in that living room, the windows were all open, the heat of day had given way to cool breezes. My mother was in an armchair and I was sprawled on the gray couch. It had been a long time since we'd watched anything together. We lived with a huge distance between us, and most of our talk consisted of her yelling for me to help with my brothers, or me yelling to her that I was going out.

"I don't think you're being fair to her," my mother said.

"To who?"

"Fair to your friend Anne. You can't keep lying and saying you're busy. You two were good friends. I don't like to see you drop a friend like that, even if she wasn't my favorite person."

I kept my eyes on handsome Steve Kiley, the motorcycle-riding doctor that shared Marcus Welby's office.

"You never struck me as mean, Gracie, and this is mean."

"Why do you care now? You and Lorine talked about her like she was a weirdo, and you were right!"

"No, no, I was wrong. And Lorine, you know her, she's Lorine. She's had a hard life."

"No, you were right! Anne's queer! She's a lesbian!"

A silence filled the living room.

My mother finally said, "There's certainly worse things."

"How can you say that? In that tone? Like it's no big deal?"

"Oh, Gracie," my mother said. "So what? She treated you nice. Remember that old friend of mine you met in Philadelphia? Theresa? She's a lesbian. I've known her since she was eight. So what."

"So what! I don't want to be her friend anymore! It is a big deal!"

"Well then, you'll have to tell her that. I will not lie for you anymore. Anne's a human being and she deserves an explanation. Every time I see her she asks about you. I really think you need to talk to her."

"I can't!"

"You're a big girl."

"Oh sure, I'm so big I can walk up to her and say, 'I don't want to come over anymore because you're a lez.'"

"I won't lie for you," my mother said. "And the word is lesbian, Gracie."

I didn't tell Anne anything. Lorine and her kids came back lobster red from Sea Isle, and another school year started, and I kissed Albie Rooch every day in the alleys of town, or on the playground at night. My father continued to work and drink and read the newspaper, my mother tended to the little kids and kept her distance. She didn't come into my room and watch me fall asleep anymore.

When I wanted to leave the apartment, I'd sneak a look into the hall, making sure Anne wasn't out there.

One day I saw her in the bakery. It was Sunday morning; I was out on my own, buying donuts. I took my number and waited in the crowd, when suddenly I heard her voice.

"Hi, Grace," she said. I turned and she was right next to me, wearing her black coat, her steady eyes devoid of the warmth I had known. Somehow in my arrogance, when I'd imagined running into her, I had envisioned she'd be more forgiving.

"Hi," I said, my face crimson and warm, and sorry.

"I've missed you," she said, "but I understand how busy you are."

"Yeah," I said, stupidly. "School and stuff."

Anne sighed with relief when her number was called. "See you," she said, and approached the lit counter. Watching her back as she waited in that bakery I was filled with shame.

It was a month or so later when I overheard my mother and Lorine one Saturday evening after the kids had all passed out on a mattress in the living room. I had been out at the playground with Albie and a bunch of other kids, and I'd come back in to check my face before we all headed to get some pizza uptown. I stood in the darkness, watching the sprawled children sleep, and listening. The pitch of my mother's voice alarmed me.

". . . and then he comes home and passes out and stinks up the room and snores beside me in the bed so that I plug my ears and hear my own scream bounce off the walls in my head. I used to go out to the couch before the kids ruined it. Now there's nowhere. Nowhere. I lie there with my fingers in my ears, trying not to breathe, knowing he doesn't love me anymore, if he ever did. Night after night, Lorine. And the days are no better."

Lorine sighed. "God, I wish I knew what to say," she said. I stood there, body frozen, heart beginning to pound throughout my entire body. I was waiting for more, dreading more, but they were silent now. What my mother had said should've been obvious to me, and would have been had I ever had the courage or inclination to extend my imagination toward her then. And yet, what I'd overheard felt both shocking and inevitable, like something I didn't know I'd always known. Now it was taking root in my heart, and beginning to break it.

"Next time around we'll be lesbian painters," my mother said, breaking the silence. "Weird lesbian gals with big white pianos and no kids."

They laughed together.

"And we'll freak out little girls like Gracie," she added.

Another laugh.

"Poor Gracie," Lorine said, sounding unlike herself. "She's got it all ahead of her."

I tiptoed past the kitchen, back to the bathroom. I would not sort it out. I'd let my mother's sorrow sit inside me, a heaviness, an ache I'd outrun. I was busy, I had places to go, I did not need this horrible interference. I yanked on the chain that turned on the bulb above the mirror. I didn't look so bad, really, I thought, reapplying my cherry lip gloss and forbidden mascara. I gave my long hair a defiant fifty strokes. My heart slammed inside me. I washed my hands, and bent to take a drink from the faucet, gulping down the cold water as if it could break through the new knowledge stuck in my chest.

I went back quietly through the living room.

"Who's that?" my mother said.

I didn't answer her then, or ever. I'd grow up never mentioning that I'd heard a word she said. I walked quietly to the door, opened it, and ran breathlessly down the stairs and into the night, as if I were free, as if after so deliberately turning away from another's suffering, the darkness of summer could ever look the same.

Berna's Place

My husband and I worked together so that the house would be presentable for our only son and his new girlfriend. "It's serious, this time," our son had told me. "I think I've found my life." Life, he said, not wife. But really, he'd found the whole package.

Jude, my husband, was a newly retired art professor, and an artist—working in oil and acrylic—and over the years our entire house had turned into a studio. We had paint thinner on the back of our toilet, smocks on the railing, art magazines piled into the corners of the dining room. I told myself this was inevitable: How could a man like Jude be contained in one room? Even the front porch had been conquered by his old cans, the dried brushes piled in a heap below the swing, the scrappy canvases he never seemed to move out to the curb for the trash collectors leaning against the wall by the door. (I'd given up.) In his art he was somewhat successful; the best galleries in Philadelphia had shown his work, and Jude was gratified by a number of fellow artists who seemed to think he was some kind of genius. Articles in the seventies about his early neo-Expressionism said as much. Though he'd never admit it, and often made the joke that he was a has-been that never was, I knew Jude *needed* to think he was a genius. In his heart he still wrestled with that tiresome affliction that most men trade in for a kind of reluctant humility by the time they turn fifty. Jude, at sixty-four, was still going strong, sometimes painting all night long in the attic, Billie Holiday or Bach for company, a view of the skyline out the window.

He was also very kind; I remember he knew I was tired from a day at work, where I sat behind a counter in a crowded hospital trying to help exasperated, sometimes furious people figure out their health care insurance. When I was mopping the floor to prepare the house for our son and his girlfriend, Jude climbed out of the cave of his work and told me to go take a nap. He'd clean, he said, his eyes still glazed with his art. And I knew he'd apply the same fierce, concentrated energy to housework as he did to his painting. The place would shine.

My son rang the doorbell that evening at dusk; I was struck by that since usually he burst through the door with no warning. I was used to him raiding the refrigerator as if he were still in high school. This night was different, though. This was the night we were to meet his girlfriend.

I was the one to answer. There they stood in the dusk, my handsome son in his maroon sweater and ponytail, a twenty-five-year-old young man who liked his dog, reading, Buddhist meditation, and hiking, and beside him, holding his hand, stood his girlfriend, as he'd been calling her, despite the fact that she was, at least compared to him, old. Sixty, I'd soon learn. Sixty. Nine years my senior. She wore a beige raincoat, and moccasins. She was very tall, with high cheekbones and lank, dark hair parted on the side, and my first thought was that she looked like my pediatrician from childhood, a woman who'd visited my home when I'd had German measles. The resemblance was so uncanny that for a moment I thought it was her, Dr. Vera Martin! I was almost ready to embrace her, for she had impressed me deeply as a child, with a sense of authority that seemed rooted both in her eloquent silences and the sudden warmth that transformed her serious face when she'd finally smile. My son's friend smiled and the resemblance only deepened.

"Hi!" I said, and stared at this woman who I knew could not be my childhood doctor, who was in fact long dead. So who was she? Not his girlfriend. Not really.

"Invite us in, Ma," said my son, and I could see he was enjoying my shock.

"This is Berna, Ma. Berna, this is Patricia, my ma."

Berna reached out to shake my hand. Her eyes were dark and warm. As she opened her coat I saw her sweatshirt was covered with decals of cats.

"I wasn't able to dress appropriately," she said. "I'm coming from work, you'll pardon me, I hope?"

"Work?"

"She's a vet," my son jumped in, beaming at her. He was more animated than I'd seen him in years. "She makes housecalls. A traveling vet. I went with her today. She's excellent. Harry—that was his dog—loves her. That's how we met. She's the only traveling vet in town." He took a deep breath; he seemed filled with a kind of desperate, nervous excitement—so different from his usual taut calm.

"A traveling vet," I said. "Well well. That's something. Please, come in, sit down."

The two of them followed me into the living room. I felt I

was dreaming. Berna sat down. She made no noise as she sat. No little groan of pleasure. No sigh. She sat with her long back as straight as the poised tails of the cats on her sweatshirt, her eyes and the eyes of the cats too alert, so that I felt like a small crowd was quietly assessing me. Griffin sat beside her, and held her hand, and suddenly I asked him if I could speak to him in the kitchen. I felt toyed with, and wanted him to know.

"Why didn't you mention she was old enough to be your grandmother?" I hadn't meant to hiss at him. In the kitchen light his brown eyes widened.

"What's your problem?" he said. "Did you turn into Dad or something?"

"Griffin, this is ridiculous! Don't act like you're not enjoying the shock value of this! She looks like my childhood pediatrician, who was old then, and dead now!"

He scrunched up his face in a sort of disgusted confusion. All the composure I'd seen for the past two years, composure that had struck me as false, had left him. I knew his palms were sweating. I felt for him, but it struck me as comical, his expecting me to take this in stride.

"I want to marry this woman," he said. "I want to marry her. This has nothing to do with your childhood doctor, or shock value." I saw he was deadly serious. So, I thought, this is how his strangeness has found itself a home. Let's hope it's temporary, a pit stop.

Berna appeared in the doorway, a tall, long-limbed sixty in a cheap, baggy cat sweatshirt that somehow was dignified enough on her.

"Look," she said. "Let's be up front here, shall we? Let's get it all out on the table. Go ahead and tell me what's pressing in on you: I'm old enough to be his mother."

"Grandmother," I said.

"Grandmother then," Berna said, with a kind of pride that

lifted her chin. "Though I'd have to have given birth at an awfully young age to make that a true statement." Her voice was soft and steady with confidence.

"I've finally brought Berna here because she's the first woman I've really loved. That needs to be known and digested."

"That's what you're telling her?" I said to him, remembering a string of girls named Cindy, and the three Jens, two of whom I'd become quite friendly with.

"I told her because it's true, Ma. Okay? Now it's all out in the open. You want a beer, Bern?"

"Sure," said Bern.

And I heard my husband coming down the steps. Here we go, I thought.

My husband and son never got along. I used to blame Jude—he'd been so absent during Griffin's childhood, so self-absorbed, and my son had been born, it seemed, awestruck by his father. Terrible combination. In those early years we lived out in the country and Jude painted in a large shed; Griffin was like a dog, waiting too patiently for the master to finally notice him and play. The more absorbed his father was, the keener Griffin's need became; Jude claimed there was something manipulative in this, but my heart broke for my child, and I think I rightly feared his very soul was being shaped by the intensity of his longing. Maybe that can be said of all children.

I'd beg Jude to give the boy a little attention, and he did, but it was the wrong kind. He'd take Griffin to the art museum. He'd try to make him memorize paintings, learn perspective, listen to facts about the artists. Griffin tried his best, and told Jude he wanted to walk into Pierre Bonnard's paintings and live there, but you shouldn't do this with a seven-year-old unless the kid is oddly brilliant, a prodigy, which Griffin never was, and I know this disappointed his father, and I know, also, that his father blamed my genes. I come from a long line of Midwestern farmers. If I said any big words in my mother's presence, she cocked her eyebrow, which meant for me to get down off my damn high horse. Intelligence was a force to be tamed into utility.

After years of rejection, Griffin finally gave up. He was twelve, then. He got a dog for his birthday that year. It seemed to me that all his love for his father got transferred onto the dog, a mutt from the shelter Griff named Roberto, for the great ballplayer Roberto Clemente. Roberto was a bit mangy and looked heartsick, but loved Griffin the way dogs love boys. A simple solution, I thought. Roberto went everywhere with Griffin—they even let that dog into the grocery store. Things were easier for Griffin after that. He became a teenager who said very little to either of us. In high school he found an enormous friend named Jack J. Pree, who wore thick glasses and who managed to attract certain girls despite his obesity. Jack lived with his aunt and uncle, drove a monstrous, ancient gold Buick, called himself the Fatso Existentialist and called Griff Brother Soul. It was the sort of mythology Griff needed. Brother Soul and the Fatso Existentialist spent days just driving around with aging Roberto hanging out the window, the three of them listening to old blues and new punk. Nights they read philosophy books aloud, or had water-balloon fights in Jack J. Pree's tiny hedged backyard, which was five doors down from us. Through a hole in the bushes, I spied on them. I loved my son, and I'd become a spy in his life.

Jude walked into the kitchen that evening, and I saw, for a moment, how handsome he was, which still happened when

I was aware that someone else would be looking at him for the first time. Griffin, Berna and I had taken seats at the oak table by the glass wall that looked out onto a little patio. Berna had first stood at the window and admired that space. "Lovely," she'd said.

"Hey, Griffin," Jude said, and looked at Berna. "Where's your girlfriend?" he said.

Berna got up from the table.

"Hello," she said. "I'm Berna Kateson." She walked over and shook his hand. She was nearly as tall as Jude.

Griffin watched them with utmost seriousness, waiting for his father to do something wrong.

"Griffin and I have been together for quite a while now, so we thought it was time to meet you," Berna said, again with her distinct, almost imperceptible chin-raising pride.

"Uh-huh," said my husband. "I see." He shot a look at Griffin, then his eyes settled on my own, and I looked down, away from him, so that he was stranded in his shock. Berna sat back down.

"I realize this isn't a typical scenario," she said. "I realize one might feel a little baffled when faced with the possibility of their son marrying an older woman, even a very successful one."

Jude opened the refrigerator and pulled out a bottle of wine, poured himself a glass, and sat down with us at the table.

"So," he said to Berna, and looked at her with coldly urgent eyes. "Why don't you tell us about yourself. About your success."

"That seems a kind of power-play question," Berna said. "So maybe I should ask it of you. Why don't you tell me about yourself? Your success?" She smiled back at him, without malice.

I could feel Griffin loving this. Her simple composure must have seemed like real bravery to him.

"Well," said my husband, "I'm sure Griffin here has told you all about me. I'm sure it's been a stellar father-son relationship report. It was all Little League and fishing trips with Griff and me."

Berna laughed, generously, I thought. Jude squinted his eyes at her, then looked at me as if to say, are we dreaming?

"We're both wiped out, actually," said Griffin. "We had a day that was hard on the heart, didn't we, Bern? I mean, we should tell the story of our day and put things in perspective, right? Rather than spend more time on this petty American bullshit?"

Whenever Griffin didn't like something he called it American. This had been his habit for years.

"We had to put two cats down, and tell a dog owner that his dog had one week of life left," Berna said. "Nobody took this well. We became on-the-spot grief counselors, which isn't unusual." She massaged her temples. She stuck her limp dark hair behind her ears.

"We?" said my husband. "Did my son go to veterinary school since I last saw him? Or is he simply Granny's sidekick now?"

"He's studying to be an assistant," Berna said. "I'm sorry you're obsessed with age, but I'd have been foolish not to expect it."

Berna sipped her beer. Then a great burst of laughter escaped from her mouth. Very, very odd. A shocking contrast to her whole bearing, which was elegant reserve.

"Excuse me," she said, as if she'd burped. Her eyes flashed, widening, her lips suppressed a smile.

"Can we go into the other room where it's more comfortable?" I said, as if we would all turn into different people if our chairs were softer.

♫

"So anyhow," Berna said, almost as soon as we sat down, "Griffin is gifted, utterly gifted with animals. By that I mean he's not only got the brains to be a vet, he's got the heart. He's already on his way to being a certified assistant, but I think that's just the beginning."

Jude sat with his arms crossed in a high-backed green chair, his eyes peering over his glasses. I sat on the couch on one side of Berna, and Griffin sat very close to her on the other side. I was really hoping they didn't do anything like kiss. Griffin had been known to kiss his other girlfriends quite blatantly, with a kind of hostile showmanship in our presence.

"It's easy to find a brain," Berna continued. "And it's easy to find a heart. I've had a whole string of assistants that were all heart. Near disasters, I have to say. The last gal, Peggy, who I thought might be good since she looked exactly like a horse—so often the ones who most resemble animals are good—I know, that's odd—but anyhow, every time we had to go to someone's house and put their pet down, she'd gallop out of the room and sob. The person losing the animal they'd loved for twenty years would be quietly welling up with tears, and then they'd stop, too concerned with Peggy's sobbing to even feel their own sorrow."

"So what happened to Peggy?" I said. I imagined her grazing in a field, chewing on hay. "Did she find another profession?"

"Peggy's all right," Berna said. "Peggy has a job in a bank now. She needs numbers. Numbers don't die."

Jude sighed. It was the sigh that said he wasn't getting enough attention.

"Before Peggy it was Michael Bent. Michael Bent turned out to be a bit of a Nazi. I suppose that's irresponsible of me, using that term when he really did nothing at all. But his eyes had me constantly on the alert. I'd never seen such icy eyes.

The eyes of an imprisoned soul. The only time I saw pleasure in those eyes was when he was giving shots. Before Michael Bent it was Darren Sedgewick, a very short, witty man in his fifties who quit a big corporate job to be my assistant, and then after three weeks died of a heart attack one evening in my car. I'm sorry to go on like this. May I go get myself another beer?"

Griffin ran to get her one; now he was back.

"Tell them about Emily Donnerbaum," said Griffin, enraptured, a child hearing stories he already knows.

"Yes, do tell us about Emily Donnerbaum," said Jude, "and then, why don't we start planning your wedding?"

A silence fell.

"How many children will you be having, Griff?" Jude said, smiling, his arms still crossed.

Griffin moved even closer to Berna. He rolled his eyes and gave his father a look of exasperation.

"You think I'd even consider bringing children into *this* world? You think I'd want them sucking down the energy of global terrorism? And as I mentioned to you a few years back, the fact that we have enough children on the globe *already* makes a *difference* to me. I'm not so big on *propagating* my own genes to gratify my own ego, which I know you think is too big, and you may be right, in fact I *know* you're right, but at least I'm trying to *subdue* it. Not to mention stray animals without homes. Why does everyone I meet have this nineteen fifties American thing about having kids?"

Griffin spoke with such passion that Jude looked at him for a moment with love. We hadn't seen any passion from Griffin for a few years. We'd seen composure. We'd heard descriptions of what he called "his practice." His practice was sitting on a pillow and counting each one of his breaths for two hours a day, before going to work as a telemarketer for Greenpeace. (He'd quit his very lucrative computer job.) His practice purified his thoughts, he said. It helped him deal with "afflictive emotion." It allowed, I suppose, for un-American transcendence.

"And we'll have a house full of animals, that's for certain," Berna said, in a voice that was soothing no matter what she was saying. "I have four cats now, and two dogs, and I've managed this restraint only because it's difficult for one person to have more than this. More than six and you start cheating them out of a superb life. But with a man around the house, especially a good man like Griff, there's no telling how many we'll be able to take in."

"Our grandchildren," I mumbled, and barked out a laugh in spite of myself.

"Actually," Berna suddenly said, looking at Griffin, "it's not in my nature to lie this way. Nor is it in yours. What were we thinking, Griff? We'd let them down easy?"

Lying?

She looked at us. "Look," she said, holding up her hand to show us the ring. "We're already married. I'm your daughter-in-law now, all right? There will be no big wedding." She smiled over at Griffin.

"Okay," said Griffin, "now you know. Bern, tell them about Emily Donnerbaum now! You gotta hear this!"

That night, after they left, I lay in bed in our dark room and started to laugh. Jude sighed, exasperated with me; this wasn't funny. In fact, each time he closed his eyes he said he pictured them in bed, naked together, and it made his skin crawl. At this I laughed harder, then settled down to scold him.

"Jude! That's rather unkind," I said. "She may be getting on in years, but she's not disgusting. Her face is beautiful. Those cheekbones I'd like to have."

"Naked," Jude said. "I keep seeing her naked, and it *is* disgusting. It's like a fairy-tale image I can't shake. I guess this marks me as pathetic and shallow. I always said you'd eventually discover this."

"No, not pathetic, Jude, but a little harsh. And in ten years I'll be her age. Will I be a fairy-tale image?"

"You'll be you."

"I think old bodies are beautiful," I said, and smiled to myself, my eyes on the twisted black branches of the tree that scraped our window. I had never really thought this before. In fact, I'd always found old bodies disturbing, male or female, but especially female. As a young woman I'd been one to sit on the beach and cringe at the old ladies walking by, I'd been one to promise myself that I'd always stay covered up when I got up in years. But in the darkness that night, remembering Berna's vivid vet stories and my son next to her, holding her hand and waiting to be alone with her, a clenched fist inside me opened up. I lay there remembering my son's waiting—the feel of his waiting—everything was boring to him near the end of our night because he wanted her, he wanted her alone, and in bed. How long had it been since Jude had experienced that sort of waiting? Waiting to have *me*? Ten years? Twenty?

"Jude?" I said.

"Mmmm?"

"I think we need to put aside our bias and learn to love Berna. She's highly intelligent, and graceful, and actually quite funny. And she brings out the *life* in Griff. Whether we like it or not, she's going to be part of us."

"You're losing your mind," he grumbled. "A young man doesn't marry a woman thirty-five years older than him. Thirty-five fucking years! If he does, the parents should step in and interpret it as mental illness, and begin looking for appropriate institutions."

"Jude! He's always been different, but he's never been mentally ill."

"I'd rather him have brought home a little bald Buddhist girl," Jude said. "If I were him right now, some part of me would be hoping my parents would step in."

"Jude, he's an adult, and he's married. We have no power anymore."

"He's a good-looking kid missing out on beautiful young women! He's missing out on the best life has to offer! He's trading all that in—the best years of his life—for an eccentric brain whose dogs probably sit in chairs at the dinner table."

Jude sat up and flicked on the light.

He looked around the room as if he'd never seen it before.

"Why would he do this?" he said, to the wall. "I bet she buys the dogs plaid raincoats like that woman we knew in Sea Isle."

"No, Jude. Berna is not the dog-raincoat type. You know that." I was exhilarated. I was, moment by moment, growing more proud of my son, and less interested in my husband, who I knew I could taunt right now—I knew I could talk to him about all the men he knew who'd left their wives and married women half their age (we had two very good friends, in fact, who'd done this, and we'd gone to their pretty, hushed, little weddings, and despite my initial cynicism I'd felt moved and happy for everyone). And I knew I could bring up Anita Defranz, a talented twenty-year-old painter he'd had an affair with eight years ago, a girl he brought to dinner after confessing the affair to me, wanting it all to be in the open, wanting me to like the girl, and I did, I did like her quite a bit even as I wanted her to vanish, even as my face grew hot at the thought of her. But I never told Jude that something ended for me during that dinner, nothing dramatic—but some part of my story with Jude *ended* as Anita Defranz told me how delicious the casserole was. "May I please have the recipe, please?" she'd said.

Jude had so trusted me to understand him, to understand his longing for Anita Defranz, who indeed was beautiful, with perfect skin and long, shiny dark hair, that I felt oddly touched by that trust, almost as if Jude were a child whose neediness made him a little dense. And now, in bed, feeling Jude's protest fill the room, feeling his confusion thicken the air in the room, I again saw him as a child, a child who could not see beyond its own sense of things. I felt sorry for him, really, and hated that pity, because it was pity that catapulted him from the realm of anyone I could unequivocally desire. Maybe I'd pitied him ever since Anita Defranz in her red silk shirt had sat so primly at our table.

"I'm going out for a walk," Jude said, pulling on his jeans. "I need some fresh air to help me figure this out."

After he left, and I was alone in the room without his protest, suddenly I was protesting myself. My one boy! This would be his life? This? How sad! Fundamentally sad, and it all must *mean* something sadder. And what kind of woman would do this? Such presumption! She was crazy, no doubt.

My sentimental visions of going to stay with his young wife after the birth of their first child, a girl, of course, the girl I'd never had myself, pressed in on me.

I wept stupid tears knowing I'd stop all this just as soon as Jude came back with the energy of his rant.

I'm a reactor, Griffin once told me, not an actor.

Jude had vaguely obsessive tendencies; it showed up in his painting (one year he painted nothing but unremarkable gray rooms with brown floors), it showed up the year he drove two miles every morning at five A.M. to get a cream donut and black coffee from Winnie's Diner, in the way he had worn only black canvas shoes by day and construction boots in the evening. He was a man who went on kicks—and I could look back over our life and organize my memories around them. *The tofu jogging year. The gambling year. The year he understood Republicans. The year of Ancient Greece books.*

And now he could not stop visiting my son and his new wife.

"Come on," he'd say, "let's go on out and see what they're doing tonight."

"We should call ahead of time."

"No," he'd say. "I want to see what they do when they're not prepared."

"That's not polite," I'd argue, but somehow we'd be on our way by then, in Jude's little Chevy, his head almost touching the ceiling, the radio tuned into a sports show—the one kick he never abandoned—and me looking out the window at the starless city night.

We'd drive nine miles into the country dark, into the wild array of brilliant stars, then up along their bumpy dirt drive-way, and we'd see the one lighted window in their house—a kitchen window—and invariably we would find the two of them on the Murphy bed—you know, those beds that fold down out of the wall, they had one in their kitchen—someone who'd owned the house long ago had nursed an invalid. So we'd look in through the window and knock and they'd call, "Come in," having no idea who we were. They were fearless; I suppose their love had rendered the whole world benign. Or maybe Berna had always been that way.

We'd step into the dimly lit kitchen. They had a Franklin stove filled with fire for heat. The air felt good. Charged, somehow, with good, unspeakable things. With spirits and spices. Both loved cooking. Griffin, I'd always thought, should have gone to chef school. He'd always seemed most happy at the stove.

"Hi," we'd say, "just thought we'd drop in and say hello."

I'd look at Jude regarding them. His face looked so troubled, all mixed up with criticism and deep interest and profound bafflement.

The two of them would be on the Murphy bed in old flannel pajamas and surrounded by three or four cats. They were always so bright-eyed, and tucked under quilts made by Berna's mother, a woman who we'd learn had joined the Peace Corps when she was seventy-four, after teaching mentally retarded adults for thirty-eight years. (My heart lurched forward, hearing this.) They'd quickly slip out of bed, smile at us and tell us to sit down at the table. In the soft light of that kitchen, with the old, creaking wooden floor and the white lace curtains and the enormous spice rack and the big cheap painting of the wild ocean, Berna looked beautiful, I noticed. Not just beautiful for an older person, but *beautiful*. Griff, who always looked perfect to me, was more so. Under the table, a black dog usually slept, snoring quietly. In the room just beyond the kitchen, a chameleon lived in a plant that touched the ceiling. To feed the chameleon Berna kept crickets in egg cartons on the solar porch in the back; she fed them powdered milk and fruits. You could always hear their song. When you closed your eyes it was as though the memory of a peaceful August night from the heart of childhood had been brought to life.

"Can I get you some tea?" Berna asked us, moving toward the cabinets.

"Tea would be good," I'd say. She had long, bare feet, and her nails were painted, which surprised me, since she wore no makeup.

"You haven't had tea until you've had Berna's," my son said.

She'd serve us ginger tea in small blue flowered teacups, with lemon and bamboo honey. It was true, the tea was better than any we'd had. She'd put the teapot on the table, and sit down. Again, I noticed how she never sighed, or groaned as she moved about, as she sat or got up from chairs. (I'd begun groaning in my late thirties.)

"So," Jude wanted to know one fall night, "where are you from, originally?"

"Nova Scotia," she said, her teacup in her hand. She had wrapped herself in an orange-and-yellow afghan.

"Nova Scotia!" he said. "Such a beautiful place."

"Indeed. I miss it every day, even as I'm utterly rooted here."

"I was there once, in my twenties," Jude said. "We hiked, and slept near the coast, and swam in the lakes. It was stunningly *gentle* land. That's my memory of it. Damn, I'd like to go back. And that wild water. Nova Scotia! I'll be damned."

"You never told me about that," I said. "I thought I knew everything."

Jude smiled at me, from a Nova Scotian distance.

Was it my imagination, or did discovering that she was from Nova Scotia change everything for Jude? He was mysterious that way—unpredictable just when you started to feel his predictability too keenly.

I remember the red leaves flying beyond the window that night, my son trying not to glare at his father, while Jude leaned in toward Berna, to hear more about her homeland, his eyes warm. She told us of her father, an old fisherman who wrote poetry and was living now in a hut by a lake. A man who coaxed the sweetest carrots out of bad soil. Berna tried to talk to all of us, but really she was speaking to Jude, responding to his own sudden interest. When Jude's interested, it's like he gets a lasso out and ropes the person in.

"We usually hit the hay about now," Griffin finally said that night, because his father and Berna were still talking about Nova Scotia, and some great, irrational fear in him was taking over all his better impulses. He was imagining the object of his desire running off with his father, of course. He was imagining they looked good together. I remembered being in that kind of love, where everyone's a threat. I was far enough away from such pain to envy its intensity.

"Griffin," I whispered in his ear as we were leaving, "relax, she loves you. Nobody is going to take her away. Most certainly not *him*."

His body stiffened at this intrusive intimacy. He had to pretend he was fearless with me. And yet, as we were pulling out of the driveway, he came out onto the stoop and waved, and I felt the wave as an offering of his thanks.

In those early months we had many evenings like this, with Berna, in her silken, dusky, calming voice, telling us stories of her family, or stories involving her work, and my son listening, marveling at this articulate, strange wonder of a wife, and watching us closely, usually. After a while he'd relax, forget to be vigilant, and we'd see his own charm as he told his own story. We'd see his youth, his thoughtful eyes, his wild energy for life, his mind, unhinged from worrying about the opinions of others (except maybe ours) and we'd understand how Berna had fallen for him.

How do I say this? Six months after I first met Berna, I became involved with a thirty-year-old groundskeeper named Abraham. Perhaps it's predictable that a mother whose son is married to someone so old would feel she's been granted a kind of license? Many would say it's Freudian, but that's too easy. I only know that after we began to accept the marriage as real, after we had seen them countless times in their Murphy bed in their eccentric pajamas, bizarre but beautiful really, with their animals and radiant regard for each other, after we had spent several Sunday afternoons walking in the woods behind Berna's house, and nights under stars she, like Jude, could name, after all that I felt a kind of penetrating amusement, a profound sort of humor infecting the whole world, and a newfound belief in surprises. I was waiting to be surprised. I was open. I wasn't walking around looking for a younger man—that sort of literal answer wouldn't have appealed to me at all. And yet, the day I visited my friend Noreen in her old home near the graveyard, I knew that when she pointed out the window at a certain groundskeeper named Abraham and said, "Isn't he adorable?" that this certain Abraham was meaningful to me, somehow. He wasn't, for me, adorable, but rather a man, and I liked his name and how he looked in the gray light, with his black eyes and his faded red hooded sweatshirt, and while it's true that I wouldn't have moved beyond a whimsical admiration of the young man had I not known Berna, I stood at the window beside Noreen and felt absolutely fired with lust for a moment. I may have blushed when she told me I shouldn't stare at children that way.

"Speaking of that," Noreen said, "how's Griffin doing with the old lady? Bernadette?"

"Berna," I said. "She's really not that old. She's younger than we are, Noreen, in a way. I mean, her spirit is roughly Griffin's age. And she's got hardly a line in her face." This part wasn't true and I was embarrassed to find myself lying. "And she moves so gracefully. I understand now, I think."

"God!" Noreen said. "I hate how everyone ends up understanding everything! It's weird, completely weird, and now you think it's normal."

I could have said, "Noreen, look at you, in this lovely old house that you keep so nice, you who fears the water and chooses to get seasick every other weekend so your husband can have his boat and eat it too, you who spends a fortune getting your hair bleached twice a month because you're terrified of looking old, look at all that and then we can talk about normal."

But I said nothing. I was not an aggressive person. I hated to hurt anyone, so avoided challenging conversation. And I was, perhaps, already planning how to talk to Abraham. I'd known Noreen for twenty-six years. We'd pushed children in strollers together. Nothing I could say would make her able to understand what I was feeling about life. She was a dear friend, but all the limits I had to respect with her made me lonely.

Abraham sat in his truck listening to music and eating a piece of bread. I walked up to the truck and said, "How long had you been a landscaper?" I was nervous, and said *had*, rather than *have*, and felt the tips of my ears grow hot.

"A landscaper?" Abraham said, "Is that what I am?"

He looked bored, at first.

"If not that, then what? What do you call yourself?"

"Abraham Horell. And you? What do you call yourself?" The boredom in his face had given way to a kind of bemused smile. It was a windy spring day, with gray light and silence surrounding us. I was aware that I'd relive this moment in memory.

"I haven't come up with a word for myself yet. Don't know *what* to call myself."

"Oh," he said, flatly, and I worried I'd been too odd.

"My name is Patricia," I said. "Some call me Trisha."

"Trisha," he said. "Nice name."

He got out of his truck. He was tall, in loose khakis. He left the music on. Miles Davis. He asked me why I was standing there at the edge of Noreen's yard. Did I know her?

"She's an old friend."

"Do you know the old man?"

"Not as well as I know Noreen."

"The old man takes her for granted. That's my opinion.

And I've only been around him three times. My father would've called him a horse's ass."

That was all I needed. It was fuel. If he could see that much, he could see a lot of things.

I looked toward the massive garden he had planted, the rich soil dark as his hair.

"You do good work," I said. And I stepped closer to him. I looked at his face. My heart was pounding because I knew that even this subtle gesture might look as wildly transparent as it felt.

"Thank you," he said, and I saw he wore a tiny star of an earring on one ear. "If you come back later, you can see the whole garden, the whole thing, finished."

"I think I will," I said. And I tried to imagine that the final look we exchanged demolished any innocence between us.

It didn't. I did come back later, and he walked me around the garden, like a proud boy with a curious parent. My heart sank as I told him how lovely it all was. I came back twice that week, and it wasn't until I brought him coffee the following week that he understood. I could tell by the way he took the coffee, brushed hair out of my eyes, lowered his chin to his chest, and held my gaze.

Later that same day Abraham and I went to a place called Ruby's Luncheonette. And I got to hear all about the sweet young man who had dropped out of med school five years ago, who was divorced, who had a child named Zoe Clare, whose ex-wife was "remarried to a rich dude" but still demanding child support, whose father, whom he'd adored, had recently died.

Abraham spoke with ease, fueled by the bad, strong coffee of the luncheonette. His legs moved back and forth under the table, knocking against each other. I didn't particularly like his style of conversation—it had that windblown quality, where you feel the person could be talking to anyone, but I didn't admit this to myself at the time.

As it turned out, we were there because Abraham lived upstairs, in a room.

After coffee, and rice pudding, and saltines, and water, up we went. My head felt full of blood. My eyes watered. I bit down on the lipstick I'd applied hours before, then wiped it off on a tissue.

You could stand at the window of his book-lined room and look down on the little main street, the unspeakably mundane workaday world, and the view gave me more reason to be there. He came up behind me, a kiss on my neck, which felt too cold, too wet, but I was relieved not to have to talk anymore, and relieved that the room was dusky, so that both my body and the pictures of his child framed on the dresser, a girl in a red hat jumping rope, were slightly muted.

"Are you on the pill?" he whispered, and I told him I was, but he should use a condom anyway—diseases, I whispered. I hadn't been on the pill for years, and the truth was, it had been two years since I'd needed to worry about any of it. The change, as they called it, was something I'd walked through as if it were a simple doorway. What change? I'd wanted to ask someone.

I did not like his kissing—too pointed, almost mock-aggressive. I kept turning my face. But soon after, when he entered me, speaking to me gently, saying, "It's okay, it's okay," and I whispered back, "I know it's okay," I did not expect to be weeping with the odd shock of joy that was simply intense sexual pleasure. I clung to him with misplaced emotion, as if he were someone I'd fallen in love with. And since no real love was anywhere in that room, save for in the face of that jump-roping little girl on the dresser, the pleasure ended in embarrassment for me.

For Abraham, I'm not sure. He may have been used to

these things. He ran down to the luncheonette and brought me up a Coke and a plate of fries. We ate them together in silence, and I kept my eyes wide on the window, and listened to the sound of my own chewing as if it could protect me from thinking things like *Here I am, a middle-aged slut!*

As I sat there dipping fries into ketchup, Jude's face, Jude's voice, broke through like a light. I was gratified to feel I missed him. Missed my husband, whoever he was.

I had four more late afternoons just like this one, and put an end to them because I understood how quickly they would put an end to themselves. Abraham's last words to me were so ironic they provoke my laughter even now. "You're wild," he'd said. How unknown I felt, but not as foolish as you might imagine.

I saw Abraham only one other time—two months later, driving through a blue day in his truck, with a dog, and a young woman, whose yellow hair streamed out the window. I honked my horn and waved, in spite of myself, and then he was gone.

"Jude," I said one night in the dark. It was raining, and we'd just watched a bad movie on television, both of us enduring insomnia. "I had an affair, you know."

"No, I didn't know."

"He was very young. He worked on Noreen's yard. It ended up meaning very little to me, but I thought I'd tell you. You've always been open with me."

"Have I?"

"As I recall, a girl you loved once ate dinner with us. She loved my cooking."

"True. True enough."

"Jude, where are you? I can't feel your reaction."

"I can't either."

"Excuse me?"

"Maybe I'm relieved."

"Relieved?"

"That you're outside the shell of this marriage when I've been outside it for years."

He sat up and put his head in his hands. I felt that he wanted to weep, but had no tears.

"Jude?" My face was red; why had I told him?

"Just don't say you're sorry."

"I won't."

"Because I've been terribly unfaithful. More than once, you know. More than twice. You probably know this. Do you know this?" I didn't say a word, but felt alone now, when I had imagined I'd already been alone. Does loneliness have floors like an endless skyscraper, and you keep descending?

"Four times. Four affairs. The last one ended last year. I've been dying to tell you."

"Really? Why don't we go downstairs and have us a drink, Jude. And you can tell me the story of our lives. You know, the one you forgot to tell me for the past twenty years or so. I'm such a good listener but you'll need to give me some details." I was on this new cold floor in the same old sky-scraper and it seemed I had a new voice to go with it, a lower, more detached sort of voice, which was the very opposite of what I felt in the dead center of my heart. It was terror I felt. Because he'd stolen my sense of our past, and I had nothing to replace it with yet.

I got all their names. Besides Anita there was Lisa, the same Lisa again a year later, Savannah, and Lily.

I sat and wrote the names down on a yellow tablet. I wrote them in a list, while Jude sat and rubbed his eyes. "Oh," he said, "Patty, I forgot Patty. She was manic-depressive."

"No, Jude, not yet, I don't want the stories yet. Just the names."

"If you count one-nighters there was also Rhonda Jean."

"Rhonda Jean," I murmured, writing it down. "Rhonda Jean! Was she a country-and-western singer, Jude? Was that the year you were always listening to Tanya Tucker?" I held the list up so he could see. "Does that look like all of them?"

He nodded. "You're stooping pretty low with this."

"Just meeting you on your own ground, Jude."

"Certainly. But it's ground well beneath you. You'll probably leave me, too, and that's understandable."

"Is that your hope? That I'll leave you?"

"No, no, of course not." He yawned, and I thought tears filled his eyes. He looked down at his own hands.

I was not ready to baby him. I took it girl by girl. I made columns for the following categories: duration of affair, age, hair color, height, weight, breast size, intelligence, family background, hobbies. This *was* beneath me, embarrassing even at the time. I was driven by an old fury finally coming to life.

The affairs had happened *before* Anita Defranz, most of them when Jude was in his thirties. Only Lily had been recent.

"So we can start there," I said. "We can start with Lily. You tell me the story, and I'll listen up."

I spoke with calm authority. I spoke in unconscious imitation of Berna.

"Lily is nobody you'd ever want to meet," he said.

"But I need the story, Jude."

"It will mortify me to tell you."

"So be it."

"She was in her twenties, she called herself a poet, I met her at Reed Carone's house, he was her professor at the time, she wore a beaded top, she was nice enough, in the summer she worked with deaf children, she was a *girl*, can we stop now?"

"Jude, it's interesting to me."

"It was physical attraction, that's all. The most elemental kind. I'm sorry. We'd go to her crummy apartment. She was a slob, and I had to endure the presence of her roommate who called me the pig. Finally the roommate said the pig could no longer enter the sty, so it was a Howard Johnson's hotel. We went there weekly for seven months. Then she fell for a young buck from Cuba, introduced me to him so I'd get the picture of how far up in the world she was moving. I was relieved. And after that I've been faithful, and will be until I die."

"Faithful."

"I certainly love you. Nobody else."

"Nice words, Jude, but who are we? I want to hate you. But then, that would be like hating my life. I don't want to do that. Do I?"

My eyes stung with tears. *My life,* echoed in my brain, and I saw myself as a little girl running down a road in Indiana, the first time I'd ever felt that sense of *my life!* I'd been stung by a bee. I remembered my father in the doorway of the kitchen, scooping me up. I cried, not from the bee sting but because I knew I had a life, and was alone living it.

"So what did Lily look like?" I said. "Like Anita Defranz?"

"More or less."

"I'd like to hate you, Jude. For all those nights you fell asleep beside me, so exhausted, so spent. You wouldn't even talk to me! I'd like to kick you, and slap you. But I'm a dignified person who is now going out for a walk."

I felt him watch me rise from my chair, and I was gratified that he was speechless.

♫

We lived in silence for nearly a week—avoiding each other when we could, and then 120 roses were delivered to my door, the card simply saying, "From Jude Harrison," which made me laugh until tears streamed down my face.

"Jude!" I hollered that day—he was upstairs painting. "Jude Harrison, this lunacy solves absolutely nothing! Where will we put them?"

He came downstairs—I stopped laughing as soon as I saw him, my heart recoiling—and together we quietly found vases and jars for each rose, and the whole house filled up with his apology. For a while, I was touched, and then not so touched. Now we had a friendly silence, sometimes broken with, "Want some scrambled eggs?" or "I need to paint in the kitchen today, if it's all right? I need that light," or "How 'bout we go see Berna and Griff tonight?"

In the car that night Jude and I rode in silence. I felt so eager to get to Griffin's house, as if it were a holiday and I were a child in love with ritual. I knew we'd be served tea, I knew they'd be in pajamas, I knew I'd hear crickets and stories, I knew the house would have that inexplicable atmosphere. *Electrified by something,* I thought, *by mystery,* I decided, though even that word did not capture what I felt there.

They had company. It was only the third time we'd come to find them not alone. The first two times it had been old Jack J. Pree, no longer a fatso or an existentialist, but married and the father of twin girls. He was still Jack J. Pree, though, full of loud laughter, and no dull judgments, and when he left he lifted Bern off the ground for a hug. His wife was more like a stunned, wide-eyed owl. You could feel her observations were grist for the mill for the tale she'd tell her friend on the phone the next day.

Tonight the company was a stranger, an old man, very old,

who we saw first through the window. I wondered if it was Berna's father.

We stepped inside; the kitchen felt like deep water. Berna's eyes were sad. Griffin was nowhere.

"What happened?"

"This is Charlie Demato," Berna said. "He's staying with Griff and me for a while."

Charlie Demato, the old man, sat at the kitchen table with a bowl of oatmeal in front of him. He had sharp elbows perched on the table's edge, and he smiled up at us. "A pleasure to meet you," he said. "You'll excuse my spirits," he added.

"We had to put down Mr. Demato's dog today. He lost his wife three weeks ago."

Jude and I expressed our sympathy. I felt we should leave. Surely Mr. Demato didn't need strangers like us. I said as much.

The old man looked up at me. "Please," he said. "Please stay. Don't go."

It was as if he were demanding that there be no more departures in life—nobody, ever again, would be leaving.

"Just sit down," he ordered.

Griffin appeared, smiled at us from the doorway.

"Berna," the old man said, "tell these people about Belle. Tell them so they know she wasn't just some dog."

Berna said that he should tell the story. That it would help him.

"Excuse me while I get my album of photographs," Mr. Demato said, and walked into the other room.

"He's staying with us," Griffin said.

"We know."

"It's part of how Bern runs the business. If some old person loses a pet and they live alone and they can't bear it, she invites them out here."

"Doesn't have to be an old person," Berna said. "Loneliness comes in all ages. A girl of twenty-two lived with me for six months one time. Turned out she had a lot to teach me. She stayed too long, she got herself pregnant, she ate too much, and made it impossible for me to meditate. But she was a teacher for me, I knew that all along."

Mr. Demato was coming back to us, his enormous album in his arms.

"Ain't I a sight for sore eyes?" he mumbled, and laughed. "This goddamn album weighs more than I do."

He sat down in the chair and opened to the first page.

"My wife, six years old!" he said, and clapped. "Deprived child. Never had a dog. Her mother claimed to be allergic. Her mother was a big liar. She hated me. My wife took after her father. Her father fell off a rooftop and died when he was thirty-two. Broke my wife's heart. Just a little girl. Never the same again."

He flipped through a few pages. His breathing quickened.

"I am unprepared," he said, "I am very unprepared. And I did many things to prepare myself. I rejoined the Catholic Church."

We were all looking at him, trying to express something with our faces. Berna was up taking bread out of the oven. I saw that Mr. Demato's hand had started to tremble. "I went into the confession booth. 'Bless me father, for I have sinned,' I said. 'But God who made death is the real sinner,' I said. The priest said, 'It is normal to be angry at death, and it's good to express your anger.'"

He looked up at us. He had urgent blue eyes. "You're all too young to understand," he said. "You live with a woman for forty-eight years. Her biggest fault is too much garlic on her food, and maybe she had to get the last word in. Bitchy once a month, even after the menopause. We got the dog sixteen years ago. A mutt. A pup. She took care of it just like it was a baby. She talked to it that way. We'd had a baby together. A smart girl. The girl grew up and moved to San Diego. The girl got breast cancer when she was forty. Survived. We lived through that together. Luck was on our side. How lucky we were. And look here, she played piano!"

He closed the book of pictures before we could see. He rested one of his hands on top of it, the other hand coming up to cover his eyes. He stood up. "I'm sorry, I am not prepared. I wasn't prepared. For the weight of it. I am sorry to go on. Berna, may I go to my room? I thank you. The dog died a peaceful death in my arms. A lovely way to go. They should do it for human beings. You have a fine son. Good night, now. The dog was named Belle."

As he walked away Jude's hand took my own under the table.

"He's a nice old man," Jude said. "I wish I'd known one good thing to say."

"Yes," I said. "Me too."

Jude squeezed my hand.

Then, the strangest thing happened. We heard the old man singing. Not softly. He was belting it out in there, a song I'd never heard. *"All the lilies, all the lilies, lighting up her face!"* He had a terrible voice, a comic voice, and who would have thought he could be so loud?

We sat and wondered if we should go to him. If this was a sign of unraveling. But nobody moved.

"The man needs to sing," Berna said. She smiled.

We ate her warm, fresh bread. *"The lilies, the lilies, the lilies in the snow!"*

We laughed a little. The song did not soften, if anything he got louder and more off-key. It went on and on. We almost got used to it.

We learned Griffin had been accepted to veterinary school in Philadelphia. We drank to that—brandy. I kissed him.

When the old man fell silent, we all rose from the table. He's sung himself to death, I thought, as we all seemed to tiptoe toward his room.

But the old man met us halfway there. He was bundled up in a parka. He said he was going out for a walk. He was going to sing in the great outdoors, he said. He was not prepared, he said. We saw he was weeping.

I wanted to embrace this man. But he was nobody any of us could embrace. He was a force for whom you simply had to get out of the way. You had to move aside and let the old man go into the great outdoors, unprepared.

We saw him, later, Jude and I. We were in our car, beginning our ride back home. The old man was headed back to Bern and Griffin's house, where he would find fire in the stove, and some companionship, and something else I don't want to shrink by naming. We didn't stop and ask the old man if he needed a ride up the hill.

"If I lost you," Jude said, "I'd be walking like that. I'd be out walking alone for the rest of my life."

His words had the near ring of sincerity, and touched me for a moment, even as I didn't believe them.

"I couldn't stand it," he said. "You're my whole life."

"Well, I hope if you sing you sound better than he did," I said, and Jude said nothing, wounded, perhaps, that I wasn't engaging his fears.

For the first time in years, I rested my head on Jude's shoulder as he drove. This was more awkwardness than it was comfort. But it was something. We rode through the dark like that, in a new kind of silence, a silence made of fading echoes, the echo of an old man's song, the echo of pain and resentment and lies that break hearts, the echo of all we'd ever meant to be for one another.

We were hungry. We stopped and had a meal in an all-night diner, Jude and I. The booth was aqua and small. We ate in silence. We could hardly take our eyes off each other. *We are what we are*, we seemed to be saying in that quiet. *We are what we are.*

We were filling up so we could go on home to continue our broken, indelicate story.

LIGHT OF LUCY

THE SOLITARY PARENTS, each in a parked car at midnight in front of the enormous inner-city high school, were mostly exhausted as they sat waiting for the ski-trip bus to pull up. This ski bus was always late, but the parents came on time anyway.

Some closed their eyes, heads back, while others stared through the dark windows into the darker Pittsburgh night as if it were an opponent who'd already beaten them down. Some leaned forward on the steering wheel and chewed gum. A few curled up in backseats, heads against doors, and when fifteen minutes had passed and the bus had not arrived, they slept, the buzz of talk radio lining their dreams, caller after caller fervently opinionated about Elian, the little Cuban boy whose mother had drowned trying to get to America.

Finally, one man got out of his car. He could no longer stand his own company in that small space. He'd had a large cup of Mini-Mart coffee; if he had to be up, then why not be truly awake? He wanted to pace on the sidewalk in the dark of this rather mild January night, and smoke. This, he imagined, might be a signal to some other parent in a parked car to get out and talk. Just some small talk. Hey, what's up? Ski bus is always late, so what are we doing here? Why can't we take the hint and show up late? He smoked, the ember blazing its orange invitation. Come on, people. Aren't we all people here? How 'bout a little human interaction? Like in the old days?

Whatta ya say? Anyone still alive?

Maybe everyone was sitting there judging him for inviting cancer into his lungs. A slovenly weakling at the mercy of a horrible appetite. "I just started smoking again last week after ten years of quitting," he considered yelling. "So wipe those superior looks off your faces!" though he couldn't see their faces. If he yelled anything at all, they'd think he was crazy. Then they'd all lock their car doors, like people had when he used to walk certain places with his black friend Darren in the seventies. Darren would say, "Watch the hands as we pass by." And you'd see all these white hands reaching for their locks, and Darren would smile sweetly at each car, and sometimes even knock on the window and shout, "Good evening!"

He hadn't seen Darren since 1980. Darren had gone west on a Greyhound with his dreams and a Chinese girl who'd changed her name to Misty.

Well look at this! A human woman is rolling down her window.

"Yo," she said, "mind if I bum a smoke?" and he said, "I don't mind at all, as long as you smoke it with me out here," and she said, "Too cold, man," and he walked over, crouched down by her half-opened window, and gave her a cigarette. His impulse was to joke her out of her car—come on, it's fifty degrees, it's a bit of spring we got here—but when he saw her face, he was glad she wouldn't be joining him. It was not her lack of beauty but her lack of restlessness that had disappointed him. Her face was so rigidly set it promised nothing, not even the drama of some private, ordinary pain that simply needed to be coaxed out of her. If she'd revealed anything, even the weighty cost of her own boredom, he would have tried. But she didn't even meet his eyes as she took the cigarette. She wore a red hat that was probably her son's, and under her big parka he noticed flannel pajamas. This touched him for a moment, and he softened. "Nice p.j.'s," he tried. She was examining the cigarette.

"Glad it's not menthol," she said and rolled up the window. He stood there for a moment before turning away.

Glad it's not menthol, he mocked silently to himself. Is that all the charm and personality she could muster on this January night? Is that all she had to spare? One life, he wanted to call to her, you got one life and this is one night in that one life, and your nights are numbered. Do you care? Do you not grasp that life could be more like the movies if only you got out of your stupid car and opened your heart, not wide, not with any degree of trust, or, hell, even interest, but rather like you open the front door for the cat, just enough for the animal to slink through into the open air?

Was everyone so tied to their own litter box they couldn't imagine it otherwise?

You could open your heart like a door for an old cat to this guy who got downsized last Thursday, to a guy whose antidepressants were finally kicking in a little—amazing, really, that a little pill could lift a giant weight a few inches off the heart—a guy who went to this very same high school twenty years ago, and if he allowed himself might be filled with despair to acknowledge that twenty years had really passed. He remembers thinking in high school that the men on his boyhood street were pathetic for hanging on to the high school football team as their source of major pleasure, remembers his own father going to the games alone with a flask of whiskey, his own father knowing all the stats of guys he himself could only watch move through the halls, guys with nicknames that seemed to come out of the air—Rocco Ramone, Lymon the Brick, the brothers McPherson, better known as Tank and Monster, and the beefy sideburns guy who called himself Unitas. They were the young brutes his father liked to spend his Friday nights on, while he himself sat in an empty South Side boxcar down by the river sharing homegrown, or the throat-scalding resin of homegrown from precious little pipes, and a case of the cheapest beer—not Iron City, but Schaefer, the one beer to have when you're having more than one—with loyal degenerates, skinny guys named things like Timmy and Fizzy and Boink, and one huge red-headed girl, Patsy Prizandance, who was a passionate athe-ist who could fix cars and quote Albert Camus. Their old tape player blasted Sly and the Family Stone or Springsteen, or old James Brown, and then later at night the Byrds and Pink Floyd. They felt so alive then! He'd go home on those nights and his father would sit with him in the kitchen, telling him all about the football game, and he'd felt the least he could do was listen to the old man, pretend to be excited, and pretend it wasn't sad, this old guy so hooked into the high school life and a job in the mill.

A job that would send every one of his five kids to college. Now, he understood. Now he himself was known to go to a high school game or two on Friday night, and what the hell, he'd say, it's damn good ball. It's cheap entertainment.

He looked at a small green car under the streetlight. A woman in that car seemed to be looking out at him.

Life could be like a movie where a sort of average-looking woman with her hood up gets out of her car and smokes with

a restless man, and the two start talking about Life itself, and
maybe the woman says, "Yeah, I'm divorced," and the man
says, "Join the club," and the woman says, "I work two jobs
and sleep five hours a night, ya know," and the man says, "I
know, and I bet you tell yourself you should be grateful,
right?" And then under her hood in the streetlight, a certain
glow on the woman's face could appear like hope. Because
here, finally, was a man who could see her as she'd been as a
child, before some crucial sense of expectation had collapsed
inside of her. "So what's it all about?" he could say, just like he
used to talk when he was sixteen, in Arby's with Matilda
Waldman, the first girl he truly loved and who loved him
back. Until she got her fine Jewish hook nose operated on. She
came back to school, the very school in front of which he now
paced, she came back the first day of eleventh grade with the
same hair, the same mouth and eyes, the same nice big-thighed
body, but her nose was Barbie's nose, and it made her a different person. "I liked your real nose a lot better," he'd told her, "it
had more, um, history." And she shrugged and said that her
new nose *was* her real nose, and that her "birth nose" had been
bad for her self-esteem, and that's why she'd been such a
burnout head with him for the past year, and really, he should
do something for his self-esteem too. Did he want to be a
burnout *head* all his life? He hadn't known how to answer
that. She said she really wanted to remain friends, but she also
wanted her freedom. "Oh, freedom," he'd said, "so you're too
good for me now without what you call your old birth nose?"
"No, no, no," she'd said, and tears of shame were in her eyes
because she knew he'd spoken some truth. She was already
popular, with her Barbie nose leading the way. He had imagined the old nose, the one he'd kissed, abandoned in some bag
of medical waste. He felt a little sick.

He'd been ruthless after that—showing her his indiffer-
ence, and once, when she'd called him crying after some

debate club Ron guy shattered her heart, he'd listened, then said, "So you want me again?" and she'd sniffed, "Sure, you're my friend."

"Friend, huh, well, I'll get used to that like the man a-hangin'," he'd blurted, and hung up, having no real idea what he'd meant by that—it was his grandfather's expression. He was a bit shocked at his coldness, but not so ashamed that he had tried contacting her again. He still remembered the sturdy streak of pleasure he felt in the middle of his regret, like a wire holding him back from the lost world of conventional decency.

If this were a movie tonight, Matilda Waldman herself would be in one of these cars, and she'd see him, and she'd come out and say, God, you look just the same except you're kind of, well, bald, no offense, and, like, forlorn-looking or something, and did you gain weight? And he'd say, You came back! You finally realized the best thing in life was to sit in Arby's with me. It struck you, in a blaze of the most exquisitely American retrospect, that life had gone downhill ever since! How are you, anyhow? Having a hard time decorating your cubicle? Need some extra Paxil? You think the little Cuban Elian will ever be able to *really* go home again?

After another cigarette he walked up to a random car and knocked on the window, his breath a cloud steaming the glass. Was it a woman? He hoped so, and it was, and when she rolled down the window, he saw it was not only a woman, it was the woman he suddenly knew he might very well have been waiting for his entire life. It was apparently, against all reason, Lucille Ball.

"Jesus," he said, "what are you doing here?"

"Oh, you know," she said, behind her sunglasses, which she briefly lifted to wink at him. Her long lashes were heavily blackened with mascara, as usual. "Desi's a ski bum," she said. "Refuses to grow up. And he wouldn't miss these trips for the world. Get in! I'm so bored. I feel I could yodel on the roof, baby doll!" She laughed. She had that same scratchy, husky voice she always had.

"Lucy!" he said. "Finally someone who understands!" He got into the passenger seat. He stared straight ahead.

"I've been watching you," she said in her husky voice.

"Watching me, huh?"

"That's right, sugar plum."

"Watching me like God, right?"

"Yes, like God. We're all watching each other like God. You know that by now, don't you, honey?"

She snapped her brilliant orange head back and laughed at this, and just then the huge ski bus pulled up. It was close to one A.M. now, and the high school students stepped down into the night, their faces beautiful because they were young and all different colors and lit by the headlights of their parents' cars, and the cars were roaring back to life, the parents pinning their eyes open. He saw his own daughter, a girl who would one day appreciate her height but who now walked like an old ape, hunched, shoulders folded inward, eyes down, brown hair like curtains on either side of her face, and what would she say when she saw him with Lucy? Did she even know who Lucy was?

"Julie!" he called out the window. "Julie, over here!"

The girl aped over to the car and her face contorted to show her father she was not amused to find him hanging out the window with a moronic expression on his face.

"Hey, kiddo, how was it?"

"What are you, like, doing in this car?"

"Take a look at who's driving, hon," he said.

The girl stooped down and looked inside. Lucy gave her a little wave. The girl did not wave back, or even smile. She had never been a particularly friendly girl, not even when she was small.

"Can we go?" the girl mumbled. "Can you say good-bye to your little friend?"

"The night is young," he said. "And Lucille Ball here might have plans."

The girl bent down again and stared. "Woh," she said, "she does look like Lucy!"

"Correction. I am Lucy."

"Isn't Lucy totally dead?"

"Really?" said the husky-voiced woman with the thick black eyelashes. "If I'm dead I'd better let your father drive."

"Dad, are you and your new friend, like, on drugs tonight?"

"Speaking for me, yes."

"Oh, this is just great."

"I'm on Paxil, like I told you. It's working. I'm alive again, the world is alive, and Lucy wants to—I don't know—what do you want to do, Lucy?"

"Let's just go for a little spin."

"A little spin," he repeated. Her voice was so perfectly Lucy's voice he had to pinch himself.

A tall boy approached the car and slipped into the backseat.

"Hey, Dez," Lucy said.

"Shit," said the boy. "Who's this?"

"This is a man named—hey—what's your name?"

His daughter leaned into the car and spoke to Lucy's son. "It's my dad. His name is Rob," she said. "He's an ordinary guy named Rob. He's also currently unemployed."

"Huh," the boy mumbled.

His mother was fiddling with the radio.

"She really does look like Lucy though," his daughter said. "I mean, who's in the trunk, Fred and Ethel and Mr. Mooney?"

"You'd better get in and buckle up," the boy said.

Lucy turned out to be a surprisingly deft driver, easing slowly into the city street now crowded with other cars of sleepy parents and skiers. She asked them all if they could enjoy a little hot chocolate from CoGo's.

"Sure," he said, and she turned on the radio.

In Pittsburgh you could always hear oldies on the radio. It was apparently the most nostalgic city on earth. Or maybe it was that way everywhere in America. The Shirelles were singing "Baby It's You"—a song popular before his time, but he knew it well, as did Lucy, who sang along huskily. "This one takes me back," she said. "New York City. Ricky despaired that year. He thought he was over the hill. Meanwhile, all the ladies on the street were dropping at his feet. It wasn't easy for me, but I sure managed well, don't you think? I still dream of Ricky, if that's what you're wondering."

"How long you two been divorced now?"

"Nineteen sixty, nineteen sixty. Were you even alive then?"

"Almost," he said, and looked into the backseat, where his daughter and Desi were half asleep, each one with their head leaning on a window.

"So you're really Lucy."

"Yep."

"All right then, name your Hollywood debut film."

"Hell, you think *you'd* know the answer?"

He was mildly aroused when she cursed.

"You got me there."

"I got you anywhere, sweetie."

She pulled into the parking lot of CoGo's.

"Nineteen thirty-three," she said. "*Roman Scandals;* what a show."

"*Roman Scandals,* huh?" It sounded improbable, or at least a bit pornographic.

"Hey, ya don't believe me, look it up. Look up my whole story. I was just a poor little girl from Jamestown, New York, and I'm still proud of it."

"As you should be," he said, entering CoGo's with her, the kids still sleeping in the car.

The store was empty except for one crazy guy talking heatedly to the money machine. And the clerk, a sallow-faced kid in his CoGo's uniform. He'd been half asleep on a stool behind the counter. Now he was off the stool, staring out the front window into the parking lot, ignoring them. Lucy led the way up and down the aisles, saying she'd know what she wanted when she saw it. "I've always been that way," she said, laughing. But they'd circled the store three times and she'd seen nothing she wanted.

"Let's just stick to hot chocolate," she finally said.

She walked up to the counter. The kid mumbled, "What's up, Lucy?" and she lifted her glasses and winked at him. "Two hot chocolates, darlin'," she told him. "No, make that four."

The kid gave them the hot chocolates in a cardboard carrier. They walked out into the night and got back in the car.

"Wake up, kids, we got some hot chocolate here."

The kids did not wake up.

"Desi could sleep through a train wreck," Lucy said. "His father was an insomniac, and I hardly need five hours a night. I don't know where he came from."

"Is that so?" He couldn't think of anything else to say. Shouldn't he have *more* to say; how many chances in life did you have to talk to Lucille Ball? Then he wanted to rap himself upside the head for thinking this could actually be Lucy. It made no sense at all, but there it was, like everything else.

"You're so quiet," Lucy said. "Cat got your tongue?"

She was headed back to the high school now, he saw, and he wished he could somehow think of an enticing detour, but already the huge brick building was looming closer. From a distance he saw his own solitary car parked in front of the school.

"The night is *still* young," he tried, as she stopped the car beside his own.

"The young are zonked," she said, nodding toward the sleepers in the back. "Better wake her up before I kidnap her. She reminds me of my own daughter."

He reached over into the backseat and shook his daughter by the shoulder. For all he knew, she may have been stoned. She peeled her eyes open and looked at him as if she found him vaguely horrifying. "Time to go now," he said, "Lucy's dropping us. I mean, she's dropping us off now."

The girl opened her door and fell into the night, then steadied herself on Lucy's fender.

"Lucy," he said, and suddenly grabbed her wrist, a very real wrist at the end of a satin shirt. "What's it all about? In a nutshell?" A memory with wings beat at the back of his neck: himself, younger, dancing in a gym.

"Oh hell, how should I know?" she said, and lifted her sunglasses quickly to wink before lowering them again. "I'm just a comedian, honey."

He paused. He could feel his daughter standing behind him on the curb.

"Good night, sweets," Lucy said. "Maybe we'll see ya again sometime."

"Lucy," he said.

"Or maybe not," she said.

"Lucy."

She waited, her eyebrows raised.

"What is it, Snookums?"

"Stay funny," he finally blurted, baffled under the streetlight, blinking back what might have been tears of confusion.

"Oh, I always leave 'em laughing," she said. "And you?"

Then she threw the car into gear, and moved off like warm silk into the cold night.

Brother to Brother

THE DAY HE FINDS A RAT behind a bag of potatoes in the kitchen cupboard is the day he calls his brother.

It was the second rat of his life in the house on Ratchet Street. He knew he should have never consented to live on *Ratchet* Street, which one of the wanting-life-to-be-fancier neighbors pronounced "Ra-Chay" Street. It was not Ra-Chay Street! Please! On Ratchet Street, a porch was always collapsing, rotten wood the outward manifestation of spiritual demise. A fat child without a coat always seemed to be out on the sidewalk, scratching his head, wiping his nose on his sleeve. The loose dogs were mangy with cold gray eyes. That kind of street.

He'd lived there eight years. His brother imagined life was a dream for him. Compared to what? Wasn't that always the question? Well, compared to his brother's life in Fishtown, life was glorious. He had, for instance, someone to love named Johnny. Johnny was a decently outraged historian and often spontaneously ordered out for Thai food. Johnny gave people nicknames. For instance, he called the man next door Besotted because the man had once asked him, "Did you know that God is *besotted* with you, even if you are a homosexual?" Now he liked it when Johnny said, "Besotted is out there watering his garden" or "Besotted parked his ugly car in our spot." It felt like enough, sometimes, to live with a man who had named another man Besotted.

When he sees the rat lurking behind the bag of potatoes, he runs out of the house with the telephone, and calls his brother. He's in his striped pajamas. He wants to tell his brother that he knows how he feels. The rat terrifies him and makes him feel defeated, as he imagines his brother must feel, always. Of course he can't use the words, "I know how you feel," because they were offensive to the brother, as they are offensive to anyone who lives in Fishtown, where despair grows like old shoes from the twisted tree branches, where loneliness claws your bare ankles when you step out of shower stalls. And if you have a window in Fishtown, it will frame sickly lightning, or tattered black clouds, and thunder often takes on the voice of the president.

You have no real memories in Fishtown, and certainly no fish. The fish have been transformed into sparring knives of shame coming up from the darkness inside of you that delights in surprising you with its endless depths. It's hard to eat because of those knives! In Fishtown, your children are the children in other lands, the dying ones. You try to send them money sometimes, but mostly you're afraid to go outside.

And so, rather than "I know how you feel," he tells his brother the story.

"I was in the kitchen, you know, just trying not to have

ADD, wondering why I'd come downstairs in the first place, and I open this cupboard, and I think to myself, potatoes. Potatoes are good. Can't argue with the goodness of potatoes. Once a friend of mine made me a nice painting of a mountain of potatoes under a midnight sky. He's currently penniless but *so* good-hearted. So I bend down and start to pick out a few nice potatoes, figuring I'd make some hash browns or home fries and think of my friend the penniless painter, when suddenly the bag moves a little, and I'm face-to-face with this big old rat, and I'm talking *big,* brother, and I jump up, and I'm shaking, you *know* how I feel about rats, and the rat jumps out of the cupboard, and starts to run across the kitchen floor, and he's like bigger than that black Buick Dad used to drive, remember, the one where we'd sit in the backseat holding on for dear life singing Jackson Five songs too loudly because he was always under the influence? So then I grabbed the phone and ran out into the rain and called you, and I don't *ever* want to go back into that house again and I *would* go to a neighbor's house but nobody on Ratchet Street likes me they think I'm a commie on top of being gay and if they knew I had a rat they'd say it was my own fault, they'd say it with their eyes, and besides, everyone's at work and I'm laid off and standing out here in my pajamas in the rain, so it's quite the lonely landscape."

What he means to say is,

> My brother, lost brother,
> Can't you see that because we clung to one another in the backseat of that black Buick in 1979 when you wore a holster and a vest with a cowboy star nothing can ever be meaningless? Our dear father drove into a field of cows and gave the cows a speech then screamed at us because we didn't laugh. And so we laughed! He meant no harm. That beau-

tiful, damaged man. And under the vest you wore
your Minnesota Vikings pajama shirt, the leaves all
around us were red clouds, and this is just today's
memory rising without reason.

Rain needles his face. To bring up their childhood would be
to take his brother's hand and press it to a hot burner. The
empty neighborhood gets emptier, as if one of the houses has
just jumped off a cliff. His brother is breathing on the other
end of the phone. He tells him he loves the sound of his
breathing.

His brother says he's glad it's good for something.

You who pummeled Raymond Brockson in the back
of St. Mary Magdelan's when he called me faggot for
the fifth time how can you think your life means nothing? Walked me home, stopping to divide your orange
and divulge your philosophy of life, your urgent analy-
sis of Neil Young's "Everybody Knows This Is
Nowhere." The essence of this day runs in my veins.

He looks back at his house, and the rat is upstairs, framed in
his bedroom window. It is all his fault for being a man afraid
like this. Afraid of a fucking rodent! All his fault. The rat
sticks his head through a hole in the screen. He stares down
at him. The rat looks interested, patient. He tells the brother
this is happening. He tells him it feels like a sign. He tells him
please, please, stay here on earth with me, you'll find your
way out of Fishtown sometime, I promise. He looks over at
Besotted's house. Closed up, curtains drawn. Where is
Besotted when you need him? He tells his brother, "We have
this neighbor named Besotted who wears a toupee and dates
a woman who is so fat she can't walk anymore. They say in
America we'll all be too fat to walk in about forty years, at

the rate we're going. I'm really looking forward to that. Really. It'll be nicely surreal. And it'll be the truth, right? I mean, we're already gluttons, so why not look the part? Right? Why should a country of hogs look svelte? No matter how much you work out, you're still an American hog, am I right?"

(He knows his brother feels accompanied when he talks like this.) His brother laughs a little. He is flooded with a warm feeling of gratitude for that small laughter.

The rat has squeezed its fat rat body through the screen. It is growing. Surprise! It is changing. We are all changing. But it is changing faster than we are. It is now a *winged* rat. That's two syllables ringing in his mind. Wing-ed. It is wasting no time. It is flying toward him in the rainy air. It is landing on his heart. Such a grip it has. How hungry it appears to be as it burrows. It is gnawing on the bones of his heart. Johnny is nowhere. The sky is racing away. He's forgotten every childhood prayer he ever knew. He is sprawled on the street now. Is this how you feel in Fishtown, he asks his brother, like a rat has landed on your heart and is gnawing on the bones and won't stop, ever again, and nothing can pry it away, and his brother comes to life and says yes, sort of, you're getting closer now, you're getting closer.

You Could Never Love
the Clown I Love

"I BET YOU'D STOP LOVING ME IF I GOT FAT," Kate said, standing in the darkened room above the Deluxe Luncheonette in Newark, Delaware. The long mirror was a silver lake on the wall. Kate rented this room and liked the place; it seemed severely romantic, and she was sick with love and fear.

And next door the clown from Baltimore was practicing his juggling act; once again the pins crashed down like thunder, and afterward the clown said, "Shit." Kate's boyfriend Thomas laughed at this. "That clown is so predictable!" he said. Now they could hear how the clown had started his act all over again.

"I wish *you* were predictable," Kate said.

"No. No you don't. You like how I bring music from Taiwan and sausages to this room. You like my bells, you like how I read you Nietzschean bedtime stories."

Kate shrugged. She thought of her father for no apparent reason. Then her mother. How small and fragile they seemed now, those people from the suburbs with their lawn pride. How sad they would be to see her in this room with a pale philosophy major who hated television.

The clown was angry again. "Shit! I'm going back to Bal-tee-more!"

Baltimore. The clown's city of origin. He couldn't help the way he pronounced it. It was how the grown-ups had taught him to say it, forty-odd years ago. The clown's real name was Rudy, and he lived on fried chicken, and so smelled like chicken, as did his entire room, his wife, Judy, and the hall-way. He bought this chicken daily from Roy Rogers, which was down on the main street of that small college town where Kate and Thomas studied and grew. Tonight was Kate and Tom's four-month anniversary; they had eaten in a Chinese restaurant, then raced home to make love, drink cheap wine, smoke clove cigarettes, and make love again.

Thomas lit a candle.

"I think we should kindly tell the clown that he was not meant to be a clown," Thomas said, because the pins came crashing down once again and startled him.

"You would," Kate said, "You *would* stop loving me if I gained thirty pounds. Wouldn't you?"

"Is that a comment on my shallowness, or yours?" Thomas said. "Can't seem to figure out the source of these pathetic questions."

"Don't torture me with your clever elusiveness! Just tell me. Would you dump me if my butt suddenly inflated to ten times the size it is now?"

He laughed. The clown's pins crashed and the clown shouted, "Pray for me!"

"Come here," Thomas said. He held her. "I would love you no matter what."

"What if I gained a hundred pounds?"

"More of you to hold."

"One seventy-five?"

"Even more. You'd be luscious."

The pins crashed and the clown said, "Damn it all!"

"Luscious? Really?"

"Really."

"What if I was so fat I couldn't fit through the door? So fat when I laid on the bed the bed just cracked right in half? Would you still love me then?"

"Absolutely. Your soul would still be inside you, wouldn't it?"

A knock came at the door. It was the clown's wife.

"Look, can you keep it down? You have these bizarre conversations, and he can't help but listen, and it's really fuckin' up his act. Excuse my mud mask."

They closed the door after assuring the clown's wife that they would try to speak more quietly. The two of them walked over to the window and peered down at the parade of pedestrians—festive tonight, moonlit, long strides eager to get somewhere, clothing bright with the colors of autumn, almost quaint, as if doom didn't rule the world.

"Would you love me if I was one inch tall?" Kate suddenly said, her eyes held wide on the starless sky.

"One inch tall?" He laughed hard at this, his eyes stinging with tears, and then settled down and said, "If you were one inch tall, I'd just keep you in my pocket."

"If I could take a pill, a pill to make me one inch tall, I would take it, and I would live in your pocket forever. I would. That would be my world. I wouldn't have to deal with the world people call the real world."

He kissed the top of her head. The pins crashed. The clown said, "Fuck this." Then it seemed he was heaving his pins at their wall.

"I thought I was whispering," she said, alarmed.

But naturally, a knock came at the door. They opened it.

"Would you love me if I was one inch tall?" Mud Mask asked them in her singsong little voice of mockery.

"I was whispering!" Kate said. "What are you doing, leaning your ear up against the wall? Can't two people in love have some privacy?"

Mud Mask shook her head, lit herself a cigarette, inhaled, exhaled, kept shaking her head. "In love," she murmured. "Is that what you tell yourself these days?"

"What do you mean these days? You've only known me for three weeks. Why is this even your business?"

"Look, my little chickadee," the mouth in the green face said. "These walls are like yay thin. In Bal-tee-more the walls are thick. We're not used to this. I can practically hear you breathing when I'm sound asleep."

"That's ridiculous."

"Lots of what's true tends to be ridiculous now, don't it, sis?"

Kate and Thomas just looked at her. They could smell the heavy odor of fried chicken being twisted and battered by the odor of her smoke. The clown's wife had more to tell them:

"I hear this conversation of yours every day, and I think to myself, can people really live that way? Would you love me if I was fat? Would you love me if I was old? Would you love me if I was one inch tall? What's next? How 'bout would you love me if I was a shoe covered with dog shit?"

Suddenly the clown appeared. He did not have his makeup on, but on his feet were the enormous clown shoes. He had grizzled gray hair, a belly, and wore a white T-shirt.

"Look, we're from Balteemore," he said. "We're not spring chickens no more. We're trying to make a living. And you two, you two are fuckin' up the whole shimmyshangin' nine yards. Every time I get the pins in the air, one of you says somethin' mental."

A silence fell. They all looked at each other.

"Okay," Thomas finally said. "We'll take a vow of silence. I mean, anything to help your pins stay in the air."

The clown turned and walked away.

"You really hurt his feelings now," his wife said. "You people understand nothing."

A feeling in the hall assured them the aging clown from Baltimore indeed had been inexplicably wounded. They were suddenly acutely aware of the clown's fragility. Within the awareness was a knowledge of their own strength, and futures, which were vast and unknown, and carried within their hearts like wild seeds. They began to feel guilt-ridden and generous, but it was too late.

"Would you love him if he was a clown?" said the clown's wife, nodding toward Thomas, and staring at Kate.

Kate nodded her head.

"Would you love him if he lived on nothing but fried chicken and cried if he didn't get his chicken at exactly the same time each day?"

"Sure I would," Kate said, and squeezed the damp hand of Thomas, her heart pounding.

"You don't know a damn thing about it," she said. "You don't know a damn thing. You and your skinny little boyfriend who reads you poems. Let me tell you somethin', college girl, you could never love the clown I love. You don't got the heart. And if you can't shut up in here, least you could do is change the subject."

But now the clown had wandered back. Oddly enough, he was smiling.

"Look," he said, his arms extended as if to embrace all three of them. "Someday we'll all be dead. So very, very dead."

The clown bent his head to the left, his eyes downcast, his lips holding a clownishly sincere smile of sympathy for all their mortal selves.

"Dead," he repeated. "All four of us. Under the ground. Gone. Isn't that some bullshit? You understand me what I'm saying here?"

"Why don't you two just come on in," Kate said.

They entered. First the clown's wife removed her mud mask in the little bathroom. She emerged white-faced and wide-eyed. Then Thomas poured them each a glass of Red Moon wine. The clown spoke of his life. He had most recently been a dishwasher. He had broken too many dishes. He had been so nervous. Things hardly ever worked out. Life was hard on the nerves, that's one thing he knew. He sighed. A silence fell, and the mystery of their breathing together deepened.

"It's good to be here!" the clown finally said.

They toasted to being alive. Then the four of them sat in a row on the double bed, their legs dangling. The clown's feet in his shoes were enormous. They laughed at that. A fire truck roared by in the street below. They listened, waiting as it passed. They sipped their wine.

THE DOG WHO SAVED HER

WHEN SHE WAS A LITTLE GIRL, she had a picture book set in Venice. The child in the book stepped out of his front door, into a little red boat, and went to see his friend.

"I want to live there," she told her mother.

"Oh!" said the mother. "Do you?"

"I do, and I will someday!"

And this story was recounted by the mother many times to others: "It was very peculiar when she spoke of Venice like that. Her eyes were shining. It was like the Virgin Mary was with us."

This was how the mother spoke in those days. She seemed unaware of her audience, who wanted small talk about the wild Maine weather, nothing more. People snickered behind her back, which pierced the observant child to the core; she hated those people, and yearned to protect the mother from cold hearts. But it proved impossible.

They left Maine, they went someplace to start over.

Philadelphia, which did not help. Her mother grew very depressed for a few years, did not wash her hair, and wore sleeveless blouses in the dead of winter. Her upper arms turned purple in the cold, as if badly bruised. She shaved her eyebrows off and replaced them with severely drawn black arches. Her gray-green eyes glazed over, and she smoked on the back stoop at night. Sometimes the child would lean out of her bedroom window and hover in the dark above her mother, trying to think of words to say that might bring her back in. Then one night she saw the mother kick an alley cat.

"Don't!" the child screamed down into the dark. The mother looked up, embarrassed. Her hands flew up to cover her face. *"Get back in bed!"* And then a long pause. And then, *"You need another mother! Not me! I can't do this anymore!"*

But the next day her Frosted Flakes were waiting for her in the dull blue bowl, as always, and she sat in the nook while her mother sat in the living room smoking in front of the television. The girl wanted to say, "You scared me last night, kicking that poor cat," but was afraid to say anything at all. She ate her cereal. Her father left for work. The house filled up with her mother's music. Tom Jones singing "With These Hands," "With these hands, I will cling to you." The mother would sit listening in a chair, as if to a lecture, her jaw thrust forward, her head nodding when she most agreed with Tom.

In school all day the girl clenched her eyes shut against the memory of the night before. The cat had screamed, sounding almost human. The girl was one of those sentimental children who refused to kill bugs, even in self-defense. She'd cried hysterically when Edgel Tosh cut a sidewalk worm in half. He'd thrown one half in her face. "It's just a stupid *worm!*"

She also had a pet mouse named Ave Maria whom she loved. She once gave Ave a ride on the Tom Jones record, around and around on the sleek blackness, a mouse merry-

THE DOG WHO SAVED HER   117

go-round. It was a secret, this ride on the record, between the
girl and the mouse.

The mouse had contracted chronic murine pneumonia
soon after that. Its breath squeaked, then rattled, its nose ran
and its eyes watered. The girl, who believed the Tom Jones
record had somehow sickened the mouse, said, "Ave needs to
go to the vet." The mother said, "Yes, she certainly does."
And away they drove! The mother wasn't the sort to say,
"Ah, she's just a mouse."

The vet, a kind man with a silver beard, gave Ave Maria a
prescription for Tylan, a good antibiotic. The mother spent
money they didn't really have. "Don't tell your father," she
warned, driving home. Ave recovered.

So. To see her mother kick a cat and kick it hard—twice—
was shocking. It changed everything, somehow, subtly but
distinctly. The girl moved further inside of herself. She
brought milk in bowls to the Philadelphia alley cats when her
mother wasn't looking, as if to repay a debt. She prayed more
than usual. For animals, for starving people. She prayed for
her mother's happiness, which finally came, but it was too
bright, too big.

The mother was so happy she smiled constantly, laughed
loudly at even the slightest joke. The girl felt the laughter
cling to her own skin. She tried to scrub it off in the tub.
"Why are you scrubbing so hard?" the mother said, and then
laughed loudly, and the sound echoed, bouncing off the tile
walls.

The mother now had orange hair, high and starchy on her
head, a red mouth, and sunglasses. She always had a mouth-
ful of Certs. It took her an hour to get dressed just to go to the
grocery store. She said to the girl, "Why do you walk like an
ape with its head down? Do you want a big hump on your
back someday?" and "Smile and the world smiles with you,
cry and you cry alone, sister!" Always beaming, and snapping

her fingers, but something brittle underneath. And when the girl wouldn't smile back: "You get that look off your face before I slap it off." And sometimes did.

But then Ave the aging mouse grew ill again. The vet said, "Mycoplasma pulmonis. I'll give you an antibiotic. Try different bedding, and avoid sawdust or shavings or hay. Shredded paper is okay."

"But I already use shredded paper. She likes her bed."

"Try CareFresh."

They tried, but Ave Maria didn't make it. Somehow the mother knew to wait before saying, "Let's go shop for another mouse." Knew, somehow, not to say, "Smile and the world smiles with you," at least for a few days. Her mother's friends, two sisters named Jean and Joan, drove over to visit in their inherited orange ambulance and took both the girl and her mother out for ice cream on Pine, and the fatter sister raised up her cone like a glass of wine and said, "To Ave."

But when the girl consoled herself the next day by wearing her cousin's hot pants and halter top, her mother slapped her face twice and called her *you little huzzy bitch* right there in front of the refrigerator, the clock on the wall like a shocked face. So confusing, the contradictions.

But who really remembers? Not the girl, who is now a young woman in faded overalls and a T-shirt. Memory for the young woman has become a surreal painting on the bottom of a sea. She doesn't dive. She's lived far from her parents for years, far enough away so that the painting is beautiful with detail that emerges in waking dreams: *mother in pink summer dress handing out orange Popsicles to the whole neighborhood.*

Mother jogging in place on the front porch watching it snow, window open behind her so she can hear Tom Jones singing "What's New Pussycat."

How she made tomato sauce. The very best.

How she took Ave to the vet.

How she worked in an office for Larry the Loser, told funny stories about him. "He thinks his ass is ice cream and we all want a lick."

Driving to a diner, late at night, after seeing Mission Impossible. "Get anything you want, sugar bird."

Polishing her red shoes.

All the betrayal, rage, and shame, all the scrubbing of the skin, the slaps and darknesses, the reasons, all gone—what painting could hold it in place?

So Julie, after several glasses of red wine, had called her mother up from Lyon, France, where she'd been living with a friend, tutoring children in English, and cleaning an old man's flat.

"Come see me! The fares are cheap! You deserve to see Europe! Come on, it's great, and Aunt Zilsy is in Paris. We'll travel. I'm on holiday!"

"Give me one good reason why I would want to visit Aunt Zilsy," she'd said, but Julie heard how her voice had inflated with hope, with a notion that she was lucky to have her daughter calling her to invite her to come to France. France! It was like the moon. But she would go. *We'll have some laughs.*

In the train station Julie had spotted her mother before her mother spotted her. Julie's heart sank as the patchwork quilt disintegrated, replaced by the wavering threads of dread, by a knowledge of her mother's vulnerability, masked as it was by the new strawberry-blond hairdo, the bright, flowery wool dress, the one hundred and eighty pounds, the pointy-toed, pointy-heeled fake cowboy boots! Cowboy boots! Since when! And she has two enormous suitcases, and one tiny one, and she's only staying for a week?

Julie wants to throw a dark cape around her mother, and send her back home.

Her mother doesn't understand the part about how everyone hates Americans.

Julie hides behind a post and watches her mother pull a compact mirror out of her expensive purse and apply her lipstick. Smack.

She waits. She breathes, then marches toward her mother. She feels the station go silent, as all eyes turn to see the American reunion.

The flowery redheaded mother envelopes her girl. Cries a little.

"I can't believe I'm here!"

The mother, up close, is childlike. The green eyes so real, so full of what passes for love. The daughter can't bear it.

"Come on, Ma," she says, and feels she'll cry. "I'll show you the apartment."

"Very clean!" the mother says. It's her highest compliment. She says it no matter where they go—even in Paris, at the Louvre: what a *clean* museum!

"Ma, did you think Europe was filthy or something?"

"I sure did!"

She does not remove her sunglasses.

In Aunt Zilsy's flat, they meet a Cambodian refugee who says his name is Bob. Aunt Zilsy (the family eccentric) has taken Bob in. Bob sort of cleans the place, and takes care of the cats, Gandhi and King. The cats slink up against the mother's legs and Julie remembers suddenly the night her mother kicked the cat *so long ago* but look how the memory collapses inside of her—and now it's all too vividly present, not just the kicked cat but childhood itself, that sickening conglomeration of that which can't be named—and what she wants is to be alone with her confusion. But her mother and Zilsy and Bob are all saying what they should do is go to Vienna. "In saucy dress," Bob says, pointing to Julie's mother. Nobody looks at Bob and says "Saucy?" A mother-daughter trip to Vienna! Bob agrees, shaking his head, even though it's likely he has no clear idea what they're talking about. He smiles, he likes the redhead lady in the saucy dress, he likes her big laughter, he nods and laughs with her since let's face it, life, at the moment, is good. Life, Bob knows, could get a whole lot worse. Looking at him, Julie decides to get over it. Just have fun!

Not so easy. In Vienna they have a barren room—beautifully barren—Julie would see the beauty under other circumstances. Now it's a prison. After a day of walking the streets of Vienna—fresh bread, good black coffee, little miniature houses displayed in a park for the coming Christmas season, a tiny bookstore where her mother had nearly shouted, "Excuse me! Sir? Sir? Excuse me! Do you have *Frommer's* guide to Vienna?" even after Julie had pleaded with her not to. Not only did they have no *Frommer's* guide, they did not speak English, and the man looked disdainfully at Julie's mother, and Julie could read his mind, how he dismissed her mother, silly American tourist, and this called up the fierce fire of her loyalty. She sneered at the man. *My mother's suffered in ways you can't fathom, miester,* says the sneer. *Get off your Viennese high horse, ya big snob!* A blatant, long, childish sneer. "Let's get out of this dump," she said loudly. (She was going a little crazy.) Maybe she'd end up like Zilsy, who never threw anything away, who sent Buddhist birthday cards to prime ministers, kings, queens, presidents, popes.

And once out of the bookstore, Julie had said to her mother, "I can't believe you just asked for *Frommer's* guide to Vienna."

Her mother laughed a little. They walked on. Silence. And then, "Julie, You're so furious with me! It's like—it's like you can't stand me!"

"It's nothing like that. I'm just tired or something."

The mother said nothing to this.

They continued their walk around the dark city.

Even without this rising tidal wave of childhood confronting Julie in the guise of her mother, it should be said that her tendency toward depression was keen, and always present. A wrestling match with depression, that's what her life had been—nothing out of the ordinary for our time. She was the sort who smelled the Holocaust in the air all through Europe, especially on the trains. And now even more so in Vienna. She'd read all of Primo Levi. Elie Wiesel's *Night*. Etty Hillesum's *An Interrupted Life*. Seen so many documentaries! *Shoah*, the whole thing, huddled alone with her boyfriend in that old college-town theater run by vets and poets. These knowledges choked her because after all she was only twenty-five, and who don't they choke, really? Her mother, she knew, could not get near that history. Her mother had no desire to wrestle with horror, no ability. Or even to admit its existence. No choking for her. It would be years before Julie would understand her mother's wisdom.

They try to sleep in the double bed in the barren room.

"I want to go home," the mother says, finally.

"I'm sorry this isn't working." *I'm suffocating, I don't know why, and I can't explain a thing. You deserve better.*

"I'll go back to Zilsy's, and fly out of Paris. Your stepfather can send me more money if I need it."

"Okay."

"What the hell is going on? Do you mind letting me in a little?"

"I don't know. I'm—I don't know."

"You don't know."

"I just want to go to Venice."

The mother sits up. Peers at the wall. "Venice," she says. "Jesus. You always wanted to go to Venice, and now you're going. You do manage to get what you want, don't you?"

"What?"

"You could be such a spoiled brat! Let's face facts."

"Whatever you say." Heart racing now.

"I didn't mean that! You weren't a spoiled brat! I'm just scared! I don't know you!"

Julie is frozen in the bed, turned on her side, looking at the opposite wall.

"It's okay," she says. "Don't worry."

Out of bed, her mother calls her stepfather. "I'm homesick," she tells him. "I'm coming home tomorrow. This was a disaster."

On the train to Venice Julie is telling strangers her name is Vanessa. Vanessa deGroot is the name she's chosen for herself. She's borrowed it from her old kindergarten teacher, whom Julie had loved fiercely at age five. Now, Julie as Vanessa deGroot on a train is no whim; it's not the fanciful play that so often takes place between strangers traveling. It's a need, a requirement born of desperation. She cannot bear to be who she is. She feels she would gag if she had to say her real name aloud. She is at the end of her rope of self.

♫

Have you ever been there? It's like you have a very high fever. You're in a room, alone, and nobody knows it. You can hear children below you playing in the street. Nobody will come to take your temperature. The fever will go on rising. Underneath the fever is panic buried by sorrow. Is there an end to the rising? You don't know. A part of you hopes to burn, burn. The bigger part wants to be saved. Wants someone, anyone, to come to the window and offer you the water of life again, in a small cup.

It's Venice now. Her dream city.

Beautiful Venice, with its squares and its alleys, its tiny streets and all those waterways, and languages clashing in the air. But the loneliness in her is so threatening everyone she passes averts their eyes, shielding themselves from her awful contagion. Can't somebody see past it? She thinks of Bob the Cambodian, steers herself away from self-pity.

It's dinner alone in a tiny restaurant. Families, babies, lovers. Outside an African man sits on a yellow blanket selling hand-carved wooden giraffes. She buys the tiniest giraffe of all, holds it in her open hand, then clenches it tightly. "A famous poet once said this is small enough to take with you when you die," says the man, and smiles up at her. His beauty catches in her throat. She puts the giraffe in the pocket of her overalls and walks on.

The gondoliers wave the tourists over to the canals. Julie goes and sits on the steps of the train station.

Night falls. She puts her head down into her arms. Her mother's face sweeps through her mind, and back again. *I'm sorry.*

And then, a dog is suddenly beside her.

It's a dignified mutt. Some black lab in there. God knows what else. It sits beside Julie, staring straight ahead. Julie looks over at the dog, then stares straight ahead as if to fathom his vision. The dog looks over at Julie. From the corner of her eye she sees this. She turns her head to see the dog's eyes, not quite looking at Julie's eyes, avoiding them the way dogs do, as if they're afraid of what they might find. The evening is lowering down, early October air like silk, cooling.

Julie moves her hand to pet the dog's back. Just a few strokes. The dog's mouth opens, a little smile. She doesn't want the dog to feel her loneliness. She doesn't want this creature to bolt. The dog's ear rises as if her touch makes an interesting sound.

"Hey, buddy," she finally says.

The dog lowers his head. She pets it. She can feel the dog's lovely bones. It wears no tags.

Soon the dog stands up and places his head in Julie's lap. This simple offering fills her with hope.

"Hey, buddy."

She'd never had a dog, but visited the neighborhood dogs when she was small, and this Venetian dog reminds her of one of those—Cookie was his name, and he was owned by the Dunnigan family, who'd lost their oldest son in Vietnam. The mother stayed indoors after that, neighbors early on would go to her window and say, "Mary, we miss you." The father would let Julie into the fence to play with Cookie. This dog here in Venice has the same gentleness, and a similar coat.

They sit together for a long time. A child approaches, asks a question in what might be Portuguese, and Julie knows the question is "Can I pet him?" and she nods. The child sits and pets the dog. Another child does the same, this one a little English girl who's been dressed to look like a sexy young woman. "Get away from that dog!" a woman calls to her. "That dog could be rabid!" And when the girl pretends not to hear, the woman nudges a man, and the man comes and scoops the girl in her tiny high heels up into his arms, and carries her away.

After an hour of petting the dog, who seems sleepy, Julie decides to test the relationship. She gets up. Will the dog get up? Yes, it will. She walks down the steps, and the dog follows. She goes back to the restaurant, and orders some beef to go, telling the dog, "Wait." She doesn't care that buying the meat means she won't be renting a room tonight. She's slept in train stations before.

When she comes out, the dog is trotting away.

"Hey!"

He stops. (It is a he, she sees now.)

"Come here, boy!"

He comes.

She feeds him a little meat, and likes how his tongue licks his chops. She's crouched down against the side wall of a tiny café now. An old man peeks his head around the corner, *"Ciao! Che c'e?!"* he says. *"Come va?"* He looks at the dog, waves them in.

She and the dog go into the tiny café, where all the old men speak Italian and drink from tiny glasses. They speak Italian to the dog, too, and buy Julie wine.

The dog gets a bone. *Bravissimo.* As if they'd been waiting for him. He chews on that, then Julie gives him the rest of the beef. They ask the dog questions in Italian. They pet the dog. They love the dog, who lays down by Julie's feet. She leans on the bar.

The only other woman in there is from Germany, older, a tall, big-boned artist named Ingeborg, and Ingeborg invites Julie and the dog to sleep in her room that night. "Two beds," she tells Julie. "And I am not there later on. I am probably in bed with one of these men." She draws Julie a map of the pensione, and shows her a large, brassy key. "I'm turning fifty tomorrow," she whispers in Julie's ear. "I am not sleeping alone tonight! Better to get some love, right?"

"Right!" Julie says, and a man gives her another glass of the most excellent wine. *"Grazie."*

He winks, makes a kissing sound.

Ingeborg and an older, smiling man with Einstein's sadly soulful eyes and a birthmark like grapejuice spilled down his neck accompany Julie and the dog across a moonlit square, through a red door, up a narrow stairway, into a dark hall. They are speaking French to one another. Ingeborg opens the door, tells Julie to leave the key on the table in the morning. Then both the old man and Ingeborg kiss Julie's cheeks, and the dog's head, and then they are gone, giggling down the steps together.

Julie smiles down at the dog. "Hey, boy," she whispers.

She is so tired. Someone outside is playing a flute. The dog is old, she realizes suddenly. His coat is still lovely enough, but the way his bones poke through, you can tell he's no spring chicken. She takes off her brown boots, her overalls, her embroidered blouse. Stands in her underwear in the dimly lit room, tiny flowers raining down the ancient wallpaper. So very quiet. The dog sits looking past Julie, out the window. It's as if the dog wishes he too could take off his clothes. A long hesitation fills the room. Julie kneels down beside him, pets him, and for the first time he makes a sound. It's almost a whimper. She stands up. Takes off her bra. Gets into the little bed under the window, props herself up on her elbows so she can see the dog, who continues to look toward the window. The moonlit dog.

"Come here, boy," she whispers, and pats the bed beside her.

The dog ignores her.

"Here, sweet boy," she says, a little louder. "Come on up."

He doesn't move. It occurs to her that he might be thirsty. There's a cup on the table, and she gets up to fill it with water in the tiny bathroom. Is very happy when the dog follows her in. She can feel his warm body against her legs. Kneels down, lets his tongue lap the water from the cup. "Just what I wanted," he seems to say. "I thought you'd never ask."

She fills it again, again he drinks, sloshing it all over her.

"Okay, now let's just get some sleep," she says, and knows the dog will join her on the bed. She slips off her underwear, kicks them off her foot, white with blue stars.

It is so wonderful, the way the dog stretches out, warm and dark, its head turned sideways on the pillow, its eyes for one moment looking into hers, then closing. *To be naked in bed with a warm, dark dog in the city of Venice.*

"Good night, boy. Sweet dreams."

He licks her face.

She kisses his head.

Feels his body, solid and close.

Says a prayer for her mother, another for the whole world.

Another for her mother.

Sleeps.

Dear Mister Springsteen

August 12, 2002

Dear Mister Springsteen,

I can hardly bear to listen to you singing on *The Rising*.

And yet I do bear it: I don't want my heart locked up, I want it torn out of my chest where it belongs, so thank you, Mr. Sprin teen.

I know nost of your fans would not address you so formally, but for me you've been like a revered teacher, and I just can't go calling you by your first name.

I've spent most of my life listening to you, and it's all been good, but this new album makes me feel I'm diving into the dark throat of the last ocean only to find a light waiting to swallow me whole.

It's you singing "But love and duty called you someplace higher/somewhere up the stairs into the fire."

I didn't know those rescue workers personally, but listening to your song, I know transcendence is real as smoke, and the music puts it deeper in my blood.

What is this pleasure we take in sorrow? Why do I stay up late into the night, spinning your CD until my whole body is one large ear? Finally I fall into a dream, where often you're waiting for me, in some dive bar with bad lighting, battered guitar in hand, glass of water shining on a table behind you. (I've been dreaming of you for almost thirty years, why stop now?) In the last dream you gave me tips on how to make my garden organic, then you rubbed ashes on my forehead like a priest.

The Rising sidles me up next to the doorway of death, and tells me that beyond that door is something wildly unimaginable and beautiful. In other words, I believe in heaven when I listen. With every song, heaven gets bigger, the sky opening and opening beyond the music.

And on this side of the heaven door, our lives with their kitchens and kisses, bloodstains and backpacks; they seem so beautifully small, like when the astronauts first photographed Earth from space.

And because certain people went up the stairs, into the fire, here I am in my living room in the middle of the night, pacing, unable to sleep, but not tired.

I've never felt less tired, Mr. Springsteen.

Had I not been up so late listening to you three nights ago, I would've missed the knock that came at my door. Normally, at three in the morning, if a knock came at my door, I'd run upstairs and spy down from the bathroom window to see who it was. If it was anyone strange, I'd not even think of answering it; I live in a neighborhood where people get

robbed, and just a few miles from a place where young people get shot in boarded-up buildings. And now that my husband doesn't live here anymore, I'm even warier, not that he
ever had a gun or anything, but I'd invested him with all sorts
of power.

But this record of yours had transported me into another
realm night after night, six nights in a row, and my kids were
visiting their father in Chicago for two long weeks, so along-
side of missing them, because of your music, my nights were
dreamy with a kind of forgiveness, and I walked in a trance
to the door and opened it to this black boy who stood looking
off to the side as if he'd forgotten what he was going to say.
Or as if he expected me to tell him why he was there. He
wore a hooded sweatshirt, despite the heat. Maybe he was
thirteen. The sight of him rendered me speechless. Finally he
looked at me and said, which in retrospect I find funny,
"Why you up?"

He was skinny, with long arms and long, beautiful hands.
He reminded me of someone. He looked over my shoulder
toward your voice in my house, as if you might appear smiling from around a corner. "Why am I up?" I said. "Because
life is short. And why did you knock at my door?" I looked
at his dark, steady eyes. I was devoid of fear; when your veins
are so filled with a certain kind of music, I guess there's no
room for fear. Besides, he just seemed lost.

"I seen the light was on."

"Then come in, sir," I said. I kept trying to figure out who
he reminded me of.

He walked into the house, his hands shoved into the
sweatshirt, his eyes big and settling on the abandoned piano
my husband and I hauled into our house last year. He walked
over to it. On top of the piano were some family pictures: my
father in front of his Plymouth, my brother in his army uniform in 1969, my husband on a bike on a rainy day, my

daughter spinning in a field the year she was three, her face thrown back to the sun.

"Why you let me in?" he said, looking quickly over at me, then turning back toward the pictures.

"Because you knocked."

"I could be a killer."

He had the softest voice.

"But you aren't. Come sit down with me. Come listen to this song." I walked over toward the couch.

"Or a crackhead." He stayed there by the piano, his head bowed down now, as if with some sudden, heavy thought.

"You're no crackhead."

"I have a gun."

"On you?"

For a keen moment my trust wavered like heat in the air between us. For that moment I knew that this music of yours had made me crazy. I was glad my kids were off in Chicago with their reasonable father. My pounding heart said I was putting my life on the line like a fool. But then he turned around and said, "No."

"So where's your gun then?"

He shrugged. His eyes flashed up at me and I saw who he must have been when he was five. One of those kids with an infectious laugh, eyes so soft and trusting they made strangers on buses stare in wonder or guilt. I could see he'd had to work hard to mold himself a mask of suspicion.

I sat down on the gray couch and tipped my head back to call him over. "Come sit down. I don't bite." He slowly walked over, took a tentative seat, waited a second, then slouched down in the lamplight as if fatigue had ordered him to do so. He smelled of night air. His body, though thin and gangly, was surprisingly still. Not like I'd expected; no bouncing leg, no snapping fingers like most boys his age. In his stillness he seemed heavy despite his slender frame, and he closed his eyes and said he was tired; he'd been out walking all night long.

"Why?"

"Because I got to." Now he opened his eyes and stole a glance my way. It hit me at once who he reminded me of. A boy named Desean who'd lived next door to my mother in Baltimore before she died. Desean Hughes, with his smart, wide-set eyes, was a fifth-grade author of a play called *Try to Be Good!* He'd told me all about it, years ago, when I visited my mother for Christmas. All these kids trying hard to be good, but it was just *impossible,* was the theme of his play.

"You remind me of a boy I once knew. A playwright."

He didn't answer. He just closed his eyes again. His weariness might have been contagious, had I not been possessed by "The Fuse."

"You like this music?" I said.

"S'okay."

"It's Bruce Springsteen."

"Who?"

"Bruce Springsteen."

His right shoulder twitched in an attempted shrug.

"You've never heard of Bruce?"

"Bruce Willis."

"You've never even heard of Springsteen? And you're from Pittsburgh?" (I was mostly teasing; I know your audience tends to be pale people who don't like their jobs much, like me.)

"Ain't from Pittsburgh, I just moved here. I'm from Allentown." Again he stole a glance at me.

"That's close enough."

"He like a country singer?"

I laughed. "No! What do you like? Rap?"

"Hip-hop and doo-wop."

"Doo-wop? What?"

"Doo-wop," he said, emphatic, a little perturbed.

"Why? I mean, how?"

"My great grandpap's a doo-wop man. He was Horace Pope. Horace Pope and the Blue Tenders, later just called the Blue Tenders."

"The Blue Tenders," I said. "Horace Pope and the Blue Tenders. I like it."

He sat up straight now, and seemed prepared to be energized. He widened his eyes. "Blue Tenders were from Allentown. They were truly famous. My great grandpap wrote all their songs."

"I like the sound of the Blue Tenders," I said. "I'd like to hear them."

"Some of the brothers is dead now."

"Still, I'd like to hear the old records."

"Hard to get. Very hard to get. Grandiose collector items."

He put his head back again and closed his eyes and I saw his beauty was a boy's beauty on the brink. I wanted to kiss his forehead, I wanted him to live in a different world. I wondered if he'd ever had to hear people say his kind was an endangered species.

"Listen to this song. Okay?"

I stood up and put on the perfect "My City of Ruins." I gave him the little book of lyrics, opened up to the last page, and he sat up and held his eyes wide and read them as you sang.

When it was over, he looked at me and said, "That's a prayer."

"That's right. You a believer?"

"Sometimes. Read the Bible, fight truth decay." Again his child eyes flashed.

"Hmmm. You go to church?"

"Back in Allentown. Sometimes now, over in Wilkinsburg." He turned and looked at me. "So why you stay up so late?"

"Why do you?"

"I got to walk."

In the distance we heard a siren.

I reached over and grabbed his hand and held it with both of mine. His eyes narrowed, he tried to pull his hand back, and I let it go. Silence. No eye contact. "Can we hear that song again?" he said.

"'City of Ruins'? Comin' up. You have good taste." I put the song on again, this time a little louder. I came back and sat beside him. We listened in silence for a while, our eyes lowered.

I thought of how I loved you, Mr. Springsteen, when I was sixteen, and took a bus all the way to Asbury Park, New Jersey, three years of listening to you already in my heart. I just walked around that town alone singing "4th of July, Asbury Park" and "Incident on 57th Street."

My husband, in the early years, used to make me tell him that story again and again.

And how the next year in psychology class Sister Berenice had us write down our peak experiences in life; we were learning about Abraham Maslow. I wrote down three things: getting a dog when I was nine, the day my brother came back from Vietnam, and the day I walked around Asbury Park, New Jersey.

Your city of ruins.

Pittsburgh's got its ruins, too.

All kinds of ruins, some you can see, most you can't.

"I got to go to Peabody High School soon," he said. He stood up suddenly, as if he suddenly remembered school was starting not in two weeks but now. He walked to the window and looked out at the dark. "You know Peabody High School?" he said to the night.

It was right down the street, beyond ugly, a typical punishment of a building. No real windows. Gunfire on the premises more than once. A failing school, as they called it.

"Looks like a prison to me," I said.

He turned around. "Exactly." He looked at me with his mouth slightly open, the faintest smile on his lips, his eyes shining.

"You're what, fourteen?"

"Fourteen on August twenty-second."

"Just a week away. I should make you a cake. Or a birthday breakfast. You want some scrambled eggs and toast with jelly?"

I put the song on again just to hear the line

"Young men on the corner like scattered leaves. . . ."

"I should go."

"Go? You just got here! Don't go."

He crossed his arms and stood regarding me for a long moment, chin lowered, eyes raised, an expression that struck me as scholarly, as he apparently weighed the pros and cons of accepting my invitation. I held his gaze, and didn't smile, pretending it made no difference at all to me whether he stayed or not. But in that moment, I so badly wanted him to stay, had he turned me down, I would've begged him to reconsider. You have to listen to this other song, I'd have said. You have to sit and listen with me just a while longer. Please don't go!

"Hungry?" I said.

"I guess I am positively hungry."

He followed me into the kitchen. I was happy. He had a quiet way of walking. I took the CD with me and put it on the little player I have on my counter. Our ceiling light was blown out, so I lit some Christmas candles (all I could find) and set them on the table, where he sat with his head lowered down and his hands folded in his lap, a posture he'd probably been taught by an adult teaching him how to behave in church.

He'd agreed with me that we should have fried potatoes with the eggs. Your music played more quietly now. I put on the song "Paradise" and I told him how you'd written the first part from the point of view of a suicide bomber.

"Nasty." He shook his head.

"If you listen, it breaks your heart. The suicide bomber's just some kid."

"Yeah, some *nasty* kid!"

"Where were you on September eleventh when you found out what was happening?"

"In school, back in Allentown."

"Math class? English?"

"In this closet by the gym with my girl."

"A closet by the gym?"

"Yeah. It was nasty, but we had an old chair down there. The janitor didn't care."

"So how'd you hear about it in the closet by the gym?"

"My girl, her stepmom called her cell phone. She was all 'the world is ending, the world is ending.'"

"So what did you do?"

"We just stayed real still and held on tight. What else you gonna do?"

"She still your girl?"

"Maybe. Maybe not. She back in Allentown." He crossed his arms, looked down.

"Here, have some juice."

"Got chocolate milk?"

I smiled at him when he asked this. He smiled back. For a moment we looked at each other. A sense of wonder had entered the room. Filled it up. For a long moment you could've gone swimming in it. I live for those moments.

"Sure," I finally said. "I have plenty of chocolate milk."

"It's good," he said, after his first gulp.

I let the potatoes fry and sat down next to him. I'd

switched on "Baby Let's Be Friends." With that one, Mr. Springsteen, innocence comes out of its grave and dances through the broken streets and all the ruins feel like manageable background.

"I like this one all right," he said. His long fingers kept time with the tune on the table, his shoulders dancing a bit.

"So tell me why you have to walk so late at night," I said.

"Because of people."

"Because of people. Okay. That narrows it down."

"Yes." He looked down. "Yes, it does. It rules out grandiose devils, and dogs." He smiled. "Can I get some more chocolate milk?"

I got him some more milk.

"Thank you, Mrs. Bruce Springsteen Lover."

He offered me a smile.

It was three-thirty in the morning. He was becoming my son.

If my husband knew I'd opened the door to a stranger in the middle of the night, he'd say I was taking a ridiculous risk and he'd be right. I'd always taken too many risks. I felt an old sense of shame wash over me.

But then this boy drank his milk down so quickly, and I realized he was hungrier than a person should be, and I got up and pushed the fried potatoes around in the skillet and told myself I will always take risks.

I remember my black friends after 9/11 said it was sort of a relief not to be seen as the enemy for a while, that for a while it was the Muslims who people had their eyes on. My black friend Veronica said she felt for the first time she was almost on the inside of America. She said she didn't like being on the inside at someone else's expense, but that was the way it felt for at least a month or so. The brown people were the enemy now, she said. What a pathetic relief.

My one friend from Pakistan, she just packed up and went

back home after she and I went to this Greek bazaar and a mentally ill woman with a flag on her shirt pushed her down on the ground like some bully on a playground. That was the end of September. My friend booked a flight the next day. She was a good friend, and I missed her. At Joe from the coffee shop's suggestion, I read Mr. Chomsky to further complicate my patriotism, which rose in me like dark sap in the shape of question marks. I prayed for the victims, for all victims, but now, looking back, I wish I'd kept praying with the same intensity I'd prayed with in September. For the victims, sure, past and present and future victims, and for the end of hatred that just keeps opening around the world like a million mouths of ugly fire. It won't be happy until it's one big mouth, one big fire, one big wasted world. (I could feel the truth of all that back then.)

But by January, life was beginning to feel mundane again. Then my husband moved out. That woke me up. Then, by May, the absence felt almost normal. I do think sometimes unless you are the one holding the dying in your arms, unless you are the one in the fire, or the one falling ninety stories down to the ground to meet your death, or truly the loved one by the side of the grave as the body is lowered, I do think, Mr. Springsteen, we all recover too quickly, which is one reason why we need these songs.

My visitor's name turned out to be Desmond. Desmond ate all his potatoes and eggs so quickly I had to make some more. He asked for another napkin. He wiped his mouth frequently, he chewed quietly, and he ate with great seriousness. This seriousness, this intense concentration, had me waiting for him to say something profound. He looked always on the verge of that. Then I realized he didn't have to say a word. He was profound enough, just being a kid alive in the world.

I know that evil is all around us. I know that I was lucky to open the door to beautiful, hungry Desmond. I know that for me, your prayer, "May your faith give us faith/ may your love give us love" is working right now.

It was hard to say good-bye to him out on the porch, the moon across the street too high, rising like a kid's lost balloon. I told him to come back anytime the light was on. "Thank you," he said, and stepped down toward the street.

"Thank you for coming by," I said.

I wondered if his black sneakers were comfortable. I wondered if he'd walk until morning. I watched him turn the corner, and some knowledge of how singular his life was, and all lives were, filled me with dread. I missed him. I missed everyone. But it was too late to call a soul. I went back in and put on *The Rising*. Obviously all you can do with dread is work to change it into love, Mr. Springsteen, and that's another reason we need these songs.

Have you ever heard of his grandfather's doo-wop group from Allentown, the Blue Tenders? They are not on the Web. Why did I think they would be?

It's hard to see those old doo-wop guys now on public TV, so innocent, so clearly from another time, so all about harmony.

I wonder who the people were that made Desmond have to walk.

I wonder what the Blue Tenders say when they talk about the world.

I wonder if someday Desmond will tell someone, "Once in the middle of the night I listened to Bruce Springsteen's *The Rising* with some white lady in Pittsburgh in her house. And she fed me. Wasn't too bad."

God bless you.

So Long, Marianne

We met when we were almost young,
deep in the green lilac park,
you held on to me like I was a crucifix,
as we went kneeling through the dark. . . .

She sang the song to Ben that spring afternoon in the store
where they worked. Her name was Marianne, like the song,
and last night, back in his room in West Philly above the little Hmong market, eating snow peas in the dark, they heard
the old song playing down in the street on a car radio. The
car was an old blue fifties' wreck with fins, the driver an
ancient Hmong man who wore a T-shirt that read *Please
Enjoy!* It was strange hearing that old Leonard Cohen song
blaring from those battered windows. Marianne's father had
listened to that record when she was a child. She could
remember him singing it in a sunny kitchen. She was twenty
now. Her father had been dead for four years.

She and Ben stood face-to-face behind the counter. The store was a health-food market owned by a woman named Nellie who decided the two of them could be trusted to tend the place while she went away. "Gotta go to Lauderdale with Karen. Gotta try to talk her outta marryin' Ron," Nellie had told them the day before she left. Nellie was short and wide-hipped, with brown eyes magnified into permanent astonishment behind glasses. Money was new to her; she liked her bracelets jangling, and she liked the audience she had in her young employees.

"Come on, you two, you know I'm right about Ron! He's South Philly Italian meets Planet of the Apes!"

She pronounced it "Eye-talian."

"I like Ron," Marianne said. She didn't, really. She liked to rile Nellie.

"Then *you* marry him! I don't want him for a son-in-law!" Her face had reddened. "Karen's father was hairless as a baby doll! Why'd she pick an ape like Ron for a husband?"

"Maybe she wants to monkey around?" Ben said.

Marianne laughed. Nellie slapped the air. "It ain't funny. He's a dropout. We had him over the house for supper, he sits at the table with his top three buttons undone, he does these bad, I'm talking *bad* imitations of the guy on *Goodfellas,* and poor Karen, what the hell does she know?"

"Nothing?" Marianne ventured.

"Less than nothing, honey. Maybe even less than the two of you lovebirds."

"If she *loves* Ron, then—" Marianne said, wanting to extend the conversation.

"You know what I say about love, don't ya?"

"Uh, no, I don't think we do. What do you say, Nellie?" This was Ben, who waited with a look of someone expecting to laugh. But Nellie only walked away, calling over her shoulder, "Don't let no lunatics in here and no charity cases and lock the damn doors at five!"

♩

That was three days ago. So far they'd obeyed all her wishes except for the charity sandwiches at the end of the day. They gave them to the homeless men and women who lingered by the door. Word spread after day one, and the next day a crowd of twenty or so had assembled. Today Marianne told Ben they should give away the flowers, too. "Why chuck 'em in the Dumpster? Homeless people might appreciate a little beauty, don't you think?"

"We'll give it all away," Ben agreed. "Bread, sandwiches, flowers. And we'll buy chocolate and give that away too. They can have a little feast. Chocolate sandwiches on French bread."

She kissed the mouth that said those words, in that voice that was painfully intoxicating to her at times. They were new lovers, two months' history behind them a red balloon they held in their hand. It threatened to cut loose at any time. Marianne leaned against his flannel chest and breathed. Her mother flashed into her mind. She was on a houseboat with a man from Florida. Marianne had never met him. She could not even recall his name.

Into the store walked a regular customer in sturdy sandals and a vivid Indian dress, her usual attire. She would buy her organic vanilla yogurt, her whole-wheat crackers. Her blond beauty was an affront; Marianne's body tensed each time she was in the store. She watched Ben greet this woman, her eyes stinging in her sockets. A woman like that—so blond and clean with no makeup at all—made her own dark hair feel heavy with oil, her attempt at eyeliner clownish. Today she watched Ben's easy smile flash more than once toward the woman, and her heart sped up. The woman paid for her goods, her steady blue eyes flashing over to Marianne, who smiled to hide her efforts at trying to decipher the secret of the woman's beauty.

"Thanks so much," the woman said to Ben, and though she was no more than thirty, it seemed to Marianne she was self-possessed like someone who had enjoyed a lifetime of serious thought and work. Someday, Marianne thought, someday will I make an impression like that on a girl in a market? A stupid girl like myself who gets wrapped like a vine around the body and soul of the man who consumes her? Her heart sank heavily for a moment. Last year she had promised to keep herself solitary and safe, far from the territory of love that had nearly killed her. Far from where she stood again now, up to her thighs in it, she thought, as she turned to Ben. He stepped forward and kissed her. She stiffened, stepped back.

"When Nellie comes back, she'll know we broke the charity rule," she said. "All those homeless people at the door. They'll be expecting stuff." She looked over Ben's shoulder at the street filled with cars.

"She'll fire us for our bleeding hearts," Marianne added. "She'll lecture us about how contagious the homeless are. She'll make us wash our hands with Ajax."

"So we'll get other jobs," Ben said. "We can paint houses with Richie Facciolo and them. We can save up and travel like we said. I'm thinking New Zealand."

She looked up at his face and found his green eyes kindly smiling down at her.

"Last week it was San Francisco," she said.

"Whatever! All that matters is we're together. And not tied down."

"Right," she said, though she heard his words as if she were older, remembering them. He was her age, but sometimes his voice was swollen with such naiveté she could only envy him.

"I've always wanted to see New Zealand. I knew an artist from New Zealand named Gwynneth who painted empty rooms. I waitressed with her last year. She'd take me home after work and let me watch her paint."

She had been strangely drawn to Gwynneth, but that she didn't tell him. Nor did she mention how long ago the memory felt. She was in love with Ben now as surely as she'd been in love with the man who had left her a year ago—was it already a whole year?—but she had a resistance inside of her, a part of her that dispelled the usual urgency to tell her story—her life story that she had told her two other loves, one after another, nights of lying by their sides in rented rooms, her childhood coming alive in the darkness so that each one could know the girl she had been, could know her fevered sense of loss.

Wasn't that what love was for? Telling each other stories? She had thought so.

The last man had extracted all her stories, his listening like a drug. She would talk and talk, then feel almost empty. Trains ran right through his backyard. They would sit up in bed and watch them, and she would weep without him noticing. He'd been older; the ghost of her father had sometimes drifted into the room on the scent of his shaving cream in the dark mornings.

Now with Ben, she didn't want her stories to fill the space between them. She didn't want her history, her memories, which had been sculpted too many times for those other loves. She wanted to be present to the present, leaving the past behind like a sealed box in the attic of a house in a dream. She wanted this love with Ben to be more about the body, less about all those words she'd always needed. When Ben asked her about where she'd lived as a little girl, about who her family was, she'd tell brief half-truths. The man with the trains in his yard had left with her stories in his heart and even if he returned now to give them back, she wouldn't want them. "Keep them," she imagined herself saying. "I don't need them anymore."

♫

"The thing about New Zealand is so much of it is still untouched."

"Untouched is good."

The store was suddenly full: the afternoon rush—the late lunchers, the vitamin people with their obsessive label-reading eyes, the doctors and nurses who needed a pick-me-up. Marianne and Ben hustled to serve them, Ben pulling fruit juice from the back room to restock shelves, Marianne at the register ringing up algae mixes, kefir, bean dips, organic chocolate bars, and fat-free everything.

She worked, she remained conscious of Ben, no matter where he was in the store. He had taken off his flannel shirt. She could see his arms in his white T-shirt, the muscles that weren't the self-conscious muscles of a health-club member, but rather his because he was Ben: a generous person who was always helping friends move in and out of apartments. A person who would stop to push a stranger's stranded car off the highway in a rainstorm. Her mind was fired by his presence, and by the oddities of the regular customers who were like actors marching across the stage of the store. Marianne didn't know if Ben's heart felt as though it would burst when these people revealed themselves, but her own did, her own heart filled with the gestures and auras of customers, and there were times when each one seemed so *sacred* (her father's word) she wanted to reach over the counter and grab a hand, touch a face, her body filled with the wild energy of wonder that any of them were here, that they existed at all.

Whenever one of their favorite customers came in, Marianne behind the counter would clear her throat to alert Ben, as she did now, because Wagon Woman was entering in her wig and purple minidress. One of the city's more visible and personable transvestites, Wagon Woman's real name was Odessa, but since she pulled friends and strangers around in a large, rumbling wood-sided wagon that recalled prairie days, much of the city thought of her as Wagon Woman. Yesterday the friend being pulled around was Harry the Dancing Stain, a skinny man with warm irony in his eyes, a man known for introducing himself as Harry the Dancing Stain without explanation. Today the wagon was empty.

"Hi, Odessa," Marianne greeted him.

"When will we get our wagon rides?" Ben called over.

"You have to stand in line, precious. I got a friend outside."

"So what'll it be today?" Marianne said.

"Four cheese on rolls and two bottles of apricot soda with a brownie."

Marianne smiled at him. "You're always so sure about what you want."

"You love me," Odessa said.

"Probably," Marianne agreed.

When the wagon rumbled out the door to the sidewalk, four or five regular customers came and went, all of them doctors and nurses infected by the brilliant spring day, a day when even in the littered city the blue air seemed to quiver with the energy of birds.

A couple of college students came in, draped around each other, obviously rich kids from Penn looking like catalogue people. The King of Fortieth Street came in singing "Solid as a Rock," the ironic theme song for a smart man who had lost his mind. He had white hair and blue eyes that were angry, amused, and proud all at once. He sang his song today looking straight at Marianne.

She thought his voice with its odd quaver was almost beautiful. She liked that he was strong enough to be in on the joke of his own insanity; that's what his eyes told her. But he was not one of her favorite customers. He singled her out with his furtive looks. He sensed, perhaps, that she instinctively understood his rage, understood that he hated himself for his wild displays even as he smiled. "You and me, girl, we're special," he said once.

"Not me."

"I can see you better than you see yourself."

"I don't think so."

"Am I hittin' too close to home?"

Her face would redden, and he'd smirk and wink, almost cruel. "Quit your job and go read Herman Wouk!" he said today, then saluted her and turned to leave.

"Who's Herman Wouk?" Marianne mumbled to the air. A nurse buying flowers shrugged and laughed.

The rush was over. Ben came up behind Marianne and pressed his lips to her neck. It sent a chill throughout her body, and for a split second she saw the face of the man who'd broken her heart. "Don't resist remembering," the therapist had told her. "The memory will get scarier. The mind's just a rebel. Tell it what to do and it wins every time. Just let the memory come, and go."

Marianne turned to Ben, and touched her hand to the side of his face.

"Let's go in the back," he said. "I'll lock up the store for ten minutes. We'll leave the sign on the door."

She hung the sign, she locked the door, she led the way, pulling him by the hand into the back room. It was small and dark and filled with boxes, enough of them already collapsed and folded up to make a bed.

They dressed, combed each other's sweaty hair, and walked out of the dark and into the store. The air held sharp little points of colored light; their legs were weak beneath them. They wanted to go back to the makeshift bed. But already the customers waited on the other side of the glass door.

The afternoon sun was deeper now, streaking across the store, orange on the far wall where the vitamins were shelved. This batch of customers, more leisurely than the lunch crowd, trickled into the store, so that when the couple with the child walked in, Marianne was ringing up a young man's bag of coffee beans and chatting with him about a pizza place. She saw the child and tried not to stare, tried to keep talking. The child was frail and bald with illness, a girl in a long-sleeved pink sweatshirt with a rabbit decal, her legs spindly under a light blue skirt that seemed made from the sky. The child glanced over at Marianne once, her face devoid of expression. The parents beside her embodied a depth of exhaustion that changed the atmosphere of the day, dark circles, taut mouths, an air of fatigue like a heavy curtain surrounding them. Marianne saw the man put his hand on his child's bare head like a firm cap for a moment.

She'd made a mistake; the customer was telling her he'd been overcharged.

"Sorry," she said, clearing her throat to call Ben over, and hardly knowing why. She rang the order again. Again she overcharged him. Her face reddened as she laughed, ringing it up a third time while the child in the blue skirt walked in front of the glass doors of the refrigerator, her reflection passing before the colored bottles of juice. The father looked suddenly at Mariar.ne, as if he thought he knew her. She handed the patient customer his bag. She lowered her eyes. She had seen all the father's human will exposed, his raw desire just to make it through the day.

"I want a Coke," the child said, pointing.

The father walked over and stood beside her. "No Coke, honey."

"I want Coke." Her voice was steady and clear as water over stones. Her voice was pure desire.

"You can pick out any of the juices. No Coke."

Now the mother walked over to them.

"I don't want juice."

"Look, hon, they even have pineapple. You love that."

"I want Coke," the child stated again, her voice even clearer, the insistence in it somehow beautiful. Why didn't they cover her head? Marianne remembered a favorite doll she'd had when she was eight, whose hair she'd chopped off, whose cloth chest had torn. Her parents hadn't had much money, but they'd taken her to a place called the Doll Hospital one autumn night.

"I really, really, really, really, really want Coke," the girl said, and Marianne felt the words lodged in her own throat. The girl repeated this, her voice rising in the store, other customers looking over at her now. The father crouched down before the child and put his hands steadily on her arms. A customer asked Marianne, "How late are you open?"

"How late are we open, how late are we open," Marianne said. "Um, six."

More customers lined up. She could hear the rising desperation of the father's voice. Now her fingers were blunt, useless on the register. "Ben?" she called out. "Can you take over the register?" The father said, "Orange, tomato, grape, apple, kiwi, pineapple, apricot. That's a lot of nice choices."

"Coke!" the girl shouted. She turned around in a circle. She looked around at the customers. "I want Coke!" she told them. And then again, louder, her voice trembling but still strong.

"Hey now, come on now, honey." The mother tried to pick her up in her arms.

Now she shouted. "I want Coke!" Any insularity the family had was ripped away. The girl had torn it, the girl was tired of her parents' protection and assurances. The child wanted them to know she knew they were lying, and she wanted her *life*, she wanted her life and was calling it Coke.

The father picked her up; she fought him. He carried her

out of the store, his eyes closed, his wife following with her chin held high. The child's desire to live was so thick in the store that Marianne rushed into the back room to get away from it. She was assaulted by the lingering scent of their love-making. She left that darkness and walked out onto the sidewalk. She could see the girl a half block away in the arms of her father, her head down now.

Back in the store they worked in silence. Marianne filled the bins of coffee for the next day. Her hands, she noticed, trembled. She could not stop imagining the girl and her parents walking past the campus toward the hospital for more tests, the tulips and bare skin of students, the laughter and daffodils and blossoming brightness of trees like claws tearing at them, the blue air stinging the child's lungs as she gulped down the day.

She was grateful to Ben for this silence. She looked over at him and smiled. He smiled back.

He cleaned the glass of the front door, and when it neared six o'clock the homeless men and women were gathering, and Ben said, "I'll take the stuff out."

"Great."

She watched them gather around him, patient as he handed out the sandwiches. She remembered the flowers and bread and chocolate and went to the door herself, setting it all outside for the taking. They scrambled forward, one woman saying God bless you honey God bless you honey over and over again. Every baguette, every candy bar, every last spring flower was gone.

Slowly they walked home together. Ben held her hand. Walnut Street was filled with kids in blaring rap. They walked to Forty-fourth and Sansom, past Wanda Jackson's porch, where little girls jumped rope and a blind man preached. They crossed the street and climbed the steps to Ben's place.

That night in Ben's room, with its light-up globe and forty-cent chairs and its mattress by the window, after canned Hmong food from the market beneath them, they held each other, voices and music below them in the street rising as if in a dream they shared together. Each time Marianne closed her eyes she saw the girl who wanted to live, and remembered herself, not wanting to live, all those months after the man who'd been like a father had told her, "It's time for both of us to move on."

For him she had come close to dying.

She closed her eyes and saw her own father's face.

This child with the bald head would live now forever in her heart's new center like a cold light.

"Tell me," Ben said, his voice tender, full of hesitation. "If you want."

She couldn't move. But words were frantic in her throat, rising slowly to enter the air, to circle around the intransmutable girl, to continue the story of who she was, who she might be.

ELIZABETH TINES

ELIZABETH TINES HAD OWNED HER HOUSE for almost twenty years now—since 1968—having inherited it from an eccentric and semifamous artist uncle she'd never known existed. She had not been aware that any blood relation of hers had been rich, much less famous, and the discovery had made her see herself differently, as if being related to him gave her potential, somehow, or would have given her potential had she known about him when she was a child living for years on canned goods, shadowed by a towering Methodist church in two rooms with her parents.

She slept now in the room where the uncle had slept, and still a painting of a woman in a red rowboat hung in a gold frame near the window on the wall—the uncle's artwork. When first she'd moved in at age forty, she had looked at the picture as a shrine, her gratitude seeming to sink into the painted water, which was endlessly deep, the appropriate container for emotion whose power transformed that part of her that had come always to expect the worst. To her the modest house, divided into upstairs and downstairs apartments, was stunning; the windows framed the hills of a city she suddenly loved, and when the fog rolled in it seemed like heavenly blankets, whereas before she had hated its ghostly persistence in softening the harsh edges of faces and battered buildings, edges that always returned when the fog retreated.

Slowly she had grown accustomed to being the owner of the blue house on the wide, flowery street, accustomed to being a landlady to people downstairs who never seemed appreciative enough of the beauty they were renting. Mostly they were young people who were products of money. They took their fashionable clothes and clear complexions and high expectations of the future for granted, and this gave them an ease that tempered their youthful energy. At their age she'd been wild to escape, hungry and watchful of everything like a skinny animal. And yet all that watching—where had it landed her?

Her marriage at seventeen to a handsome thirty-year-old man obsessed with betting on horses had lasted two years, and then, pregnant and on her own, she had worked for Mad Maids, Inc., cleaning houses with two older women named Connie and Bonnie who suggested she go by the nickname Jonny just for the sake of the business. So she had, she had become a Mad Maid and taken a boy's name and each day life was good because Connie and Bonnie said it was good, and they all met in their uniforms every morning at dawn in a little café that looked out over the Pacific, where Jonny would sit on the round stool between the older women at the counter trying to dream up a future she could believe in. Despite the baby growing inside her, she'd had so many visions then—herself as pediatrician, herself as modern dancer, stewardess, so she could travel—she entertained all possibilities.

"You're smart, girl," Bonnie would say, whenever she tried

to speak of the future. "You can do anything you want, can't she, Connie."

It was because she liked words; Connie and Bonnie had never heard words like "ludicrous" and "countenance" and "rendering."

"Hell, you could be a lady rocket scientist one day for all we know."

But her own heart had been unable to hold on to the roots of her dreams; they dangled in space, then vanished. Moments came when she was suddenly overcome by fear so powerful she wanted to cry out, and so laughed too loudly, her face reddening when the false voice echoed in her head. She would swing violently into a region of self-contempt, seared by these feelings that seemed to her like revelations. "Yeah, I'm about as smart as a bowling ball without any holes," she'd say. "And as lucky as the alley it's rollin' down."

Years passed. Elizabeth worked, tended to her child, a wiry boy named Curtis, and slept. She did other things too—went to movies, bars, read magazines, fell in and out of love with men who were versions of her long-ago husband—obsessed men, self-involved men, addicted men whose love for her ran out after five or six months. For years she drank coffee with a woman who lived across the street, and the friendship gave her real pleasure, but she worked long hours, and her life was essentially a routine she endured. "Girl, you're one of us," Connie and Bonnie started to say to her, and there came a day when she stopped hearing the irony and embraced it as a compliment. She began to feel she belonged with the women, that it was her lot in life. She had cut herself off from her parents, and even when her son began to look like her father, she had little desire to see them again.

♩

And now Elizabeth was sixty, still called Jonny, though Connie and Bonnie were both dead. She worked alone, with a concentration that made cleaning a kind of meditation. The quiet days went fast. She did not mind the work because she knew she could quit, knew she could survive on the money she made as a landlady, if necessary. Her son had grown up and married a woman from Pennsylvania; they lived there, childless, content to be so. He was a decent man, warmhearted, but so busy on his little farm, so full of his feeling for the land he tended, visits were few and far between. He would call, expecting her to make him laugh with some story from her life, some little observation she had made. "The woman whose house I'm cleaning now has twin ferrets," she'd say. "How am I supposed to clean with a couple of asshole ferrets on my heels?" she'd add, if the ferrets themselves weren't amusing enough.

She broke her ankle one day walking down Clayton Street after working in a pink Victorian. It hurt badly; she limped home in her white dress and white shoes, sweating with pain, and Bennet, one of the downstairs tenants, was outside on the front stoop with a glass of orange juice. He got up and helped her, though he himself, she knew, was thin because he was sick. She had known that the day he'd shown up to rent from her. His face had struck her immediately with what looked like willed happiness, but a dry rope of fear had risen in her throat when she considered his illness; they were always finding out new ways you could catch it, weren't they? And would he be bringing his friends around? But she had surprised herself by speaking through that fear and reaching another part of herself, not out of any allegiance to her own sense of morality, but as an instinctive response to the young man, whose silent presence was so oddly kind.

"The place is yours," she'd told him that day, after showing him the rooms. And he had commented on their beauty and order as few tenants did. "You really keep this place nice," Bennet said. "Honey, I was born to keep places nice," she told him, and saw his eyes darken with amused interest.

And now, her ankle throbbing as he helped her up the steps and into her living room, she was acutely aware of the strength in his thin shoulder, and aware of herself as a woman who hadn't touched another human being in years. How did that happen? she wanted to ask someone in that moment. How did it happen that a woman like me went for years untouched?

In his old blue Chevy he took her to a doctor an hour later, waited while her lower leg and foot were wrapped in a cast, and on the ride back home suggested she lay her head back and rest. But she felt she couldn't; she felt she ought to repay him somehow, or at least aim to entertain him a bit.

"So you like my perfume? It's called Lysol."

"Sexy," he said. "You like your job?"

"Do I like being an interior sanitation engineer? Hell yes, wouldn't you?"

He laughed. "What's the best thing about your job?"

"Sometimes I get the windows so clean I make them cry," she said. "That's one helluva moment for me."

He laughed again.

"You're all right," she told him, and a silence settled into the car.

As he drove for a moment she turned to watch the side of his face, and saw a naked expression in his eyes that made her think of a child. She turned back to the road, remembering his touch as he helped her up the path. She wanted to reach over and touch his elegant hand on the wheel, and felt herself fill up with wonder in the face of this small, odd desire.

♫

Months later they sat in his kitchen, Bennet with a vivid green scarf around his head, both of them in thick sweaters. Outside late autumn rain fell through fog. A candle was lit on the round table. They drank tea from a blue pot with the moon painted on the side of it—a gift from Bennet's sister Anne, who came by once a day, serious-faced in her bright skirts and sandals. Elizabeth had cleaned his apartment all morning, and now the tile floor and surfaces of the wooden counters gleamed.

"You know, Bennet," she said, "I like cleaning your place better than anyplace I've ever cleaned."

"I'm not sure what to say to that," Bennet said, teacup in hand. He smiled, then adjusted his scarf, pushing it up on his high forehead. He looked especially thin, with lesions showing on his neck and the side of his face.

What she'd meant to say, and would never feel comfortable saying, was that he had changed her life somehow, in some important way that she could not articulate. He'd done it with the ferocity of his kindness, with the trips he'd made to the market for her after she'd broken her ankle. With the flowers he left on her steps that he got from his friend, whose job was delivering flowers. And most of all with the easy way he spoke with her, right from the beginning, as if he really saw *her,* and not just a landlady-maid with dyed red hair and a cracked voice to go with her hands.

Now, in his kitchen, she felt loosened to talk, to tell him a story she'd never told anyone else.

"You know, Bennet, I was raised up in Kentucky by crazy Holy Rollers until I was fourteen. The only gay man I knew in that whole town was a poor man who ended up killing himself on New Year's Eve. I think it was 1947. His name was Joe Beehan. I'd seen him every morning in the luncheonette where I went with my father for coffee the year my father had some money. Joe Beehan would sit in a booth by himself and eat alone in his dark shirts and when he looked up at me, he'd smile. I thought he was the handsomest creature around. God, he was handsome. He was a movie star."

"Do you know why he killed himself?"

"Oh, who the hell ever knows anything. But I do know he was discovered with a man at three in the morning in the alley by Reiner's hardware store. I imagine it was all over for him in that town after that."

"Never love a man in an alley by a hardware store," Bennet said.

"I remember how my parents acted after reading that news in the paper. Seemed to me they weren't a bit sad. They were calmer than usual. They said, 'Now that's no surprise, is it, dear?' 'Not at all, Dorothy. Nothing makes a man so unhappy as walking down Sin Street. The real shame is he won't ever see the Lord's face.'"

"And when I said, 'Why not?' they said, "'Elizabeth, suicides sin against the Holy Ghost. The only face they get to see is their own. A suicide has to look in the mirror for the rest of time, Elizabeth.'"

"My God," Bennet said. "Isn't that a sweet little story."

"Very sweet for a twelve-year-old girl. What did I know? I became interested in suicides after that. I'd walk by Mr. Beehan's house every evening and look in the windows at his old bed and dresser and two pictures of a man framed on the wall by a blue wooden chair. I never have told anyone this story, Bennet. I hardly knew I remembered it so well."

"Was there anything else in the room?" Bennet said.

"Don't think so."

"I bet you wanted to climb in."

"I did. I wanted to climb in the window and lay in his bed. I wanted to lay in his bed and look at the moon shining in his mirror and try to feel what it was like to be him."

"I can imagine."

"It was odd. I took snow from his yard and packed it in a jar and kept it under my own bed until my mother or father dumped it out."

"Snow from his yard?" Bennet said. He had interest, not mockery on his face. He shifted in his seat and leaned forward, his sharp elbows on the table's edge.

"Don't ask why. Maybe I thought I was taking the ground he walked on. And then every night before I slept I'd think of him, and how he must've felt in the car waiting for the old carbon monoxide. I'd just lay there and think of him and the damnedest thing was it was like I was falling in love with the man."

"I'd say you had good taste for a girl, Jonny," Bennet said.

"So sometime that year I developed a logic that said it's better to kill yourself and be alone forever than be with a God so mean he couldn't understand the human urge to get out of this crazy world."

Bennet nodded his head.

"You know?" she said.

"I think so," he said. "But I'd be just as scared to be alone for all eternity."

His face had darkened. He looked down at the table. She was suddenly intensely ashamed. Speaking of death this way to a young man who'd have to face it much sooner than she would. She hardly knew now why it had seemed important to talk to him like this. To let him know that somehow at twelve years old she'd had a quirky wisdom, a certain feel for the suffering of others. To let him know she'd lost that wisdom along the way, but that knowing him, the sheer force of his kindness, had reminded her of who she might have been, had fear not ruled so much of her life.

He had to take a nap, he told her, after one more cup of tea and moments of silence that for Elizabeth were awkward.

"Well, it's been nice chatting, as usual," she said.

"As usual, come again," Bennet said, walking her down

the hall to the door in his thick purple socks.

Upstairs Elizabeth paced around her own kitchen and dining room, smoking, unsettled inside, for she was not accustomed to confiding such old memory to anyone, not even herself. She walked to the mantel, where pictures of her parents stood framed before the mirror. Both shots were uncharacteristic: her father smiling with his head cocked to one side, a man of thirty in a summer breeze, plaid shirt wind-whipped around a vigorous body; her mother with the neighbor's puppy on the back stoop, wearing a sleeveless dress printed with apples and pears, long teeth sunlit as they bit down on her lower lip as if to keep from laughing. These were handsome lies, and they had never become more than that for Elizabeth, who must've imagined that choosing these shots to frame could have somehow diminished the real memory of their cruelty, which sat like a locked room and had been there forever; a cold fact, intransmutable, mostly left alone.

She sat on a chair by the window now, and closed her eyes, thinking of Bennet, of how he would pick his friends up off the ground when he saw them, wasting his strength, overflowing with energy whose source was strictly spiritual at this point. She thought of the day months ago when he'd come toward her out on the sidewalk with the same joy, and she had feared that intimacy and backed away, saying, "Hello there, Bennet," sounding and feeling so much like her mother in that moment she had lost her breath.

And what would Bennet have said today had she continued her story, told him the end of it, how she'd been beaten with a belt until her legs and back bled, two days after her mother had shown her father the small red diary where she'd written about Mr. Beehan and God? Beaten until she felt she had frozen for good from the inside out.

♬

Elizabeth did not visit Bennet again for a while; he had many other visitors, and he was growing weaker; she could see that from her window when he walked up the street from the N-Judah. She had seen him riding in the cable car twice, once with a man who held his hand, once when he sat alone, his eyes peering out at the landscape as if trying to drink it up.

Lately she left food on his steps, fresh bread from the Tasahara, and oranges and notes saying to call on her if he needed something.

One day as she was leaving the house of one of her employers, the woman stopped her at the door.

"Say, Jon, did I see you talking with Bennet McGee the other day in front of your house?"

"I don't know, did you?"

"Is it possible?"

"Sure. He's a good friend."

"Really? Really? Oh my God! That's just wild! He is so wonderful! He and Barry and Jed were so much fun at those council meetings!"

"I'm sure," Elizabeth said, noticing the woman looking at her differently, trying to figure out why a man like Bennet would have her as a friend.

"That guy—oh, man, it's always the really beautiful guys who get sick. It's like you feel someone like Bennet should escape it, but the nicer they are, the more doomed they seem, or something."

"Seems to me the guys who aren't so pretty get sick too," Elizabeth said.

"Oh sure, sure, you're right. God, I feel helpless, like I never know if I'm doing enough."

"Well," Elizabeth said, "none of us are ever doing enough. Ain't that the story of the human race?"

Her employer laughed as she stepped out the door into a brilliant day.

♫

Three days before Christmas Elizabeth sat on the ledge by her bay window facing the street. Bennet approached the window in a huge black overcoat and a cowboy hat he wore for humor. But he was not funny. He was so thin, so white, that Elizabeth had to look away. But he came up to the window and smiled at her, an old man.

"Want to come in?" she said, and didn't wait for his answer. She hurried to the front door. "Come in," she said. "Come talk."

"I have to catch a flight home. For Christmas. I just wanted to wish you a happy holiday."

"Oh, well, that's nice. I'm glad you're going home. Oregon, right?"

"Got any plans?" he asked her.

Bennet's sister pulled up in her small white car.

"Not this year. I'll take it easy this year."

"Come to my house! Come with Jack the flower man! My parents' house, I mean. The Cascades and everything."

"Oh, no. Oh, no, not me. I don't travel."

"Call Jack. He's driving tomorrow. He needs company or he falls asleep. I love Jack, Jonny. I don't want him falling asleep at the wheel and you could keep him awake."

"Or put him to sleep even quicker," she said and laughed. But to her great surprise, she was imagining it.

"Look up Jack Verona. It's in the book."

His sister was out of the car now, placing Bennet's suitcase in her backseat, along with a bag filled with wrapped presents. How did he manage it all?

"Come on, Ben," she called. "We gotta go. Hi, Jonny!"

Elizabeth waved. She was glad he had this sister, whose face fought grief with a determination that verged on rage. It kept her efficient and dependable.

They drove off.

♫

Elizabeth drank scotch that night and called Jack the flower man while listening to pop songs on the radio in the dark. She left a message on his machine, and the next morning he called her back.

"Can you be ready, like now?" he said.

"Sure can," she said, surprised that she'd have no time to change her mind. She hadn't been out of the city in decades. She did not really want to go, and yet here she was, packing an overnight bag with great care, and looking around the disheveled apartment for prized possessions to take with her, as if she were going away forever. Her shelves were crowded with little trinkets and statues, her tables crowded with magazines and pieces of odd material, and she decided she had no prized possessions. It came as a mild shock, for she had a collector's nature.

The night sky was packed with stars that nearly touched the Cascades, the snow shining brilliantly in the blue light of a nearly full moon, the silence in the valley made deeper by the low-pitched whistle of wind. Elizabeth stepped down out of the van into the landscape, pulling her coat tightly around her, her bones stiff from the long ride with Jack, whose black lab had sat between them like a patient child, watching the road. Jack and Elizabeth petted the dog, told stories of dogs, talked to the dog, and it had been enough.

"We just walk down the path here and then the house will appear. Follow me," Jack told her, his bearded face blue-white in the moonlight.

"I climbed that with Bennet once," Jack said, pointing to the mountain. "He was so fucking *quick*."

The house was a stone bungalow with a slanted roof, the windows brimming with light.

"Come on in," said a man's voice, and suddenly in the front hall Bennet's father took their coats, and Bennet approached them using one crutch to walk. He still had the black coat on. He looked ancient, and happy.

"I can't believe you came!" he said to Elizabeth. He stared at her. She wagged her head. "First time I made a trip in forever," she said, smiling at him, smiling around the room and trying to get a sense of where she was.

It was a big family; soon children flocked around Bennet as he sat on the couch. A small yellow-haired girl in red overalls kissed his face.

Elizabeth had found a seat near the Christmas tree; its bulky size dwarfed her as she sat back. The warm room was all hard wood and old furniture and framed photographs on the walls. Bennet kept calling across the room, introducing her to people.

"Excellent that you came!" his brother said, and crouched down by the chair to chat. "So how'd you get a name like Jonny?"

She told him the story, making it quick and funny. Then Bennet's aunt was handing her a scotch. "How 'bout something to eat?" she said.

"No, I'm just fine, I'm just fine."

She was overwhelmed to be in a room where so many people were hugging each other, holding each other's hands, laughing and talking and tending to the fire. She felt the depth of the family's intimacy and history filling the house, and looked at them all from a great, warm distance, filled with admiration, but also with an intense awareness of Bennet. She could feel how he heightened the mood, and framed the night in sorrow so deep nobody got near it. It was the single dark current running through the living room's center; they tiptoed over it, and each one laughed louder, talked more, in order not to feel the current rising. Sorrow had a smell like metal that cut through the scent of pine and hot cherry pie.

"Here's your pie," a lovely girl told her, handing her the plate.

"Thank you."

Elizabeth was watching Bennet's mother, who much of the evening had played the piano, singing, grandchildren flanking her. Now she stole a look at her dying son as he spoke to his ten-year-old nephew on the steps that led to a loft. Elizabeth watched the mother watching Bennet and saw what looked not like sorrow but raw hunger in her eyes, a hunger for her son's whole life. She got up from the piano and called out, "Who needs what? A drink? Whip cream for the pie?" and Elizabeth looked away, feeling she had seen too far inside her.

The room where she tried to sleep was cold, but under several quilts she was warm. Her bed was aligned near the door, facing the window. The white mountains were more than a light in the room; they were a voice. A low, heavy voice that sang to her. In beds on the other side of the room three others slept—two adults and a child. Elizabeth had gone to bed earlier than they had, pretended to be sleeping, and had watched as they quietly slid themselves under the covers.

After the house settled into silence, hours seemed to pass, and Elizabeth waited for morning, when sunlight would blast through the rooms. Later, she could head back home.

But for now she was a woman in a house filled with the stunning voice of the mountains. And after another hour she was a woman in flannel pajamas leaving her bed, a barefoot woman quietly walking down the dark hall toward the living room, where she had heard some other sleepless soul moving about. She hoped it would be Bennet, then felt guilty for that hope; he should be sleeping, he should be drinking deep sleep like medicine.

But now she was at the end of the hall with a view of the living room, where Bennet stood before the sliding glass doors, still in his coat, a blanket draped over his head like a scarf. Should she whisper his name? Walk toward him, stand beside him? Talk to him, somehow? Or should she leave him alone, turn back and find her bed again?

Her body was frozen in place; her hand pressed hard against the wall. "Bennet? It's Jonny. Are you all right?"

"Jonny," he said.

His head was bowed down into his hands.

Her body did not move, but her heart, her spirit, whatever it was that filled her, rushed toward him and surrounded him so that she felt she had no choice but to follow it, to go to him, to say his name and feel her own trembling hand reach out to his shoulder. "Bennet, Bennet."

"I can't face up to what I'll never see again," he said. She felt herself a small child in his arms as he turned toward her now, the black coat opening just enough for her stunned head to lay against his chest in the absolute darkness of love.

STADIUM HEARTS

WERE SOMEONE TO APPROACH ME SOMEDAY and demand
that I define myself, as best I could, in one sentence or less, I
would not need a long sentence, nor any time to drum up a few
choice descriptive words such as "demanding," or "tender-
hearted," or "brutally honest," all of which would be true in some
sense, the way that almost anything said about anyone can be true,
given the complexities and vagaries of the human character.
Instead, I would simply say, "I am a man who loves to drive."

I'm retired now from a small college, where for over twenty
years I played the role of a basically decent though hard-nosed
professor of philosophy, a thin, appropriately wild-haired aging
man in a long dark coat, known for extracting from my students little wisdom teeth they never knew they had, and
spilling the quiet drama of my lectures into the voids of their
hearts, even when words in my mouth felt like mothballs,
though real mothballs, I knew, had much greater purpose.

I was probably never cut out for the job. Like most, I

began in a state of feverish desire to leave the mundane world and enter the world of ideas, a desire whose source I know now was a kind of self-loathing.

Having nothing to do with the college anymore, I wake up early each morning, dress, and walk out to my car, a ghastly old gold tank of a Buick I found for three hundred dollars two years ago. I stop at the donut store where the girl with green hair hands me a large cup of coffee and a newspaper, then gives me the condescending wink some young women like to give old men. But I like her. I imagine she is weary of her job, but she displays none of that.

First I drive to a hilltop that overlooks the river. I park in a lot behind a green tilted-looking greasy spoon called Rudy's, and I sit and read the paper and drink the coffee and look down at the water. You are no doubt thinking I'm a man of considerable nerve to be stealing your time like this simply to tell you how I begin my day. But how I begin my day is now essential to me, and dictates what happens during the rest of the day; when fueled by black coffee and the paper, I drive, usually on the highways, listening to a local talk show, enduring the relentless drill of loneliness without a trace of self-pity. In this world, things happen to you when you're lonely that simply don't happen otherwise.

What happened to me will be hard to describe, and yet I feel a tremendous need to try. You may want to close your eyes, like a small child in a narrow bed. There is no glowing clown night-light in this room that scares you, no ruthless, drunken parent refusing to keep the door open. Nor will this story give you bad dreams. Perhaps it is just a story of coincidence, but I don't think so.

It became apparent to me that I had to climb a certain fence. I spotted the fence from the window of my car as I was driv-

ing in the early afternoon on the empty freeway. You might
not find it strange that such a thing would become apparent
to me; after all, fences beckon climbers every day. And I am
not such an old man, really, so one needn't conjure the image
of a spindly, depleted crab clutching onto cold links with
blue and desperate hands. One might argue that this rising
urge to climb the fence was not that extraordinary, that contained within the "very being of a fence" (I am no phenom-
enologist) is a loud invitation to people like me, who, as you
might have gathered, have natures that are in some sense
"fenced out" of this world, and by no means do I pretend to
suggest that such a nature is rare or admirable. Quite the
contrary.

From the highway I seemed suddenly to see it for the first
time. It was not poetic. It did not inspire memories of past
fences, which I would've resisted. It was the thing itself, the
cold gray links in the autumn light. The car was warm, and
suddenly I resented its comforting confines. I wanted my
hands on the fence.

This particular fence happened to surround the stadium,
the large, modern stadium where baseball is played. There
are men who easily made the transition from the old, intimate stadiums, men who embraced Astroturf the way others
after them would have to embrace video screens and the
increasingly prolific assault of meaningless noise. I am not
one of those men. I regret this now, for had I been less reac-
tionary, I would have enjoyed more evenings of baseball with
my wife and son, neither of whom are living anymore. The
two of them would go along without me, after my son begged
and tearfully pleaded with me to join them, after I answered,
as usual, "I have to catch up on some reading." Finally his
mother would grow understandably disgusted, and drag him
off, saying, "Let's leave your father to his brooding,
Lawrence." This is not my son's real name; I would not call a

child Lawrence. I prefer not to speak his name aloud like this, which you will understand.

I parked the car on a side street, got out of the car, buttoned my coat, put on my hat, and crossed the freeway while a terrific gust of wind seemed to push me in the direction of my desired destination. I had to hold my hat down. Usually such a wind would irritate me; I am not a man who likes to be pushed. But at the time I thought only, What a strong wind. And now it seems strange to me, like a gift from nature, as if nature itself was propelling me toward the fence.

I climbed the fence slowly. My arms shook, and my hands hurt as I climbed, grabbing onto the links. I imagined the people driving by on the freeway, holding me in their minds for a moment, then letting me go. I worried that a cop might sight me, but not as much as I would have worried had I been younger. My white hair, my lined face, the skin that sags around my eyes, all of these protect a person from having to explain himself. Nobody expects it, and nobody's interested. Easier for them to conclude that you're nuts. You're climbing the fence because you've gone round the bend. You're having a delusion. You're climbing to get next to the stadium because you loved Ted Williams too much, or Clemente, or Willie Mays, or Vida Blue, or your son the baseball fan in his backward red cap and buck teeth and darting black eyes. The cop might have said, "Hey there, hey, grandpa, what's up?" Or would a cop today perhaps be frightened even of a respectable-looking old white-haired man climbing a fence, as if that old man might turn and pull a loaded gun out of his coat pocket, and fire the gun just to feel a part of society?

If purity of heart is to will one thing, then I had purity of heart as I continued my climb. Once on the other side, I stood and examined my hands; they were red and raw-looking, and still shaking, and I looked at them in a kind of scientific wonder. My heart hammered away at my chest. I dropped my hands down to my sides and began to walk toward the stadium. On the ground level a series of long white doors stood in a line like a group of doctors. I walked by the doors, not interested in them enough to try opening them.

Soon I found myself slipping under a metal bar that blocked a ramp leading to the heart of the stadium. I could hear the soft soles of my shoes thudding against the concrete as I walked up the ramp through a cold hollowness, while a part of me lingered behind, watching, thinking, and nearly saying aloud, *What are you doing here? Where do you think you're going?* We all make these efforts to turn into policemen when the police don't show up. But I was not about to stop and answer that voice; I was not capable. I was occupied by a need to collect myself, to force myself into a suitably solemn state of mind, as if I were approaching a great occasion of some sort, an occasion that demanded the heart, not the body, be appropriately dressed. As I ascended the ramp I could look to my right at the city skyline, frozen in the gray autumn sky, like a world I was leaving behind.

Soon I was on the top floor. The place was emptier and colder somehow than anyplace I had ever been before. I tried, briefly, to imagine my son and wife here, lost in a shuffling summer crowd, the boy begging his mother to spend five dollars on a pennant, his mother refusing, the way she knew I would refuse, the boy knowing not to press the issue. The two of them would walk along, not holding hands, not needing too, for they would never lose each other. Between them was a bond that was palpable in the air, as if their very bodies extended beyond what I could see with my naked eye, as if there were no space at all between them. They would be the quietest people in the stadium; the boy's eyes watchful, serious, lit with intelligence I couldn't see, and his mother's eyes blue and introspective, though somehow seeing everything around her at the same time. The boy in his faded black sneakers, a cheap glove on his hand in case a ball came his way.

I continued walking. I whistled for a moment, just to hear the echo. A strange bird in a stadium, lost. *What are you doing?*

I badly wanted to look at the field.

Up here was another series of doors, and they were locked; I tried six of them, and gave up. But then, as I was walking away, thinking I would return to my car and a more reasonable version of myself, I decided to try one more door, the seventh door, which opened easily, mysteriously, so that I was almost fearful.

Now I was inside, and much to my disappointment, I looked down and saw that the field was covered with a dark green plastic. What had I been thinking? Of course it would be covered. Our great nation's splendiferous Astroturf needs protection from the elements, stupid man!

Surrounding me were thousands of orange and yellow plastic seats, dabs of paint in the vast silence, the haunted emptiness that told me I had better turn around and head back down the concrete ramp. Instead, like a man with a ticket stub, I walked over to section D-5, and took a seat in aisle 3, a seat in the middle of that aisle. I sat and folded my hands on my lap. I sat there in silence and looked down at the covered field.

I became aware of something remarkable. I mean to say another person was in the stands, a bit higher up than me, in a yellow section, on the other side, above what should have been the third-base line.

My first response was to get up and run, but I am never a man who acts on his initial sense of things. And so I sat and stared across at my company, who from that considerable distance seemed to be a woman, neither young nor old, in a blue coat. Surely she had seen me, and surely she was finding this situation as odd as I was, yet she seemed oddly comfortable. Together we sat in that emptiness for twenty minutes or so, and it became apparent after the first five minutes that we were staring at each other. It was difficult to *see* that, but in a space so empty it was quite easy to *sense* it, for there was little else to sense, save for the ghosts of summer. I began to wish that I smoked, for I would certainly have smoked at this time, and with an ember burned a hole in what was becoming the acutely surreal fabric of my day.

Some more minutes passed, when finally the woman made her first gesture, which amounted to a rather ornate wave, as if she imagined herself in a parade, on a float. The fluidity of that wave I could never describe. It was a wave that demanded nothing from me, not even that I wave back, and so I was moved to do exactly that, though my wave was sharper, perfunctory, and embarrassed. I'm not a man who could wave like I was in a parade even if I was in a parade. As soon as I waved, she stopped, and as if with a will of its own, my hand flew up and waved again, the same short wave. She did not return this wave with a wave. Instead, she did something that I would have to describe as wonderful, in the original sense of that word.

She stood up on her seat.

I sat there and watched her standing. I smiled, irresistibly, for this gesture was like a child's. Who else stands on chairs? Always it is children, attempting to reach something they need, and always they are told to get down. *Get down off that chair!* If they refuse to get down, someone yanks them down, and leaves a red mark on their wrist. This woman stood stone-still for a while, and then she wrapped her arms around herself.

It was then that I stood up on my chair. I cannot explain the emotion that overtook me when I was standing and facing her across that distance. This time I waved first, and she waved back, immediately, and quickly. We stood there for no more than ten minutes like strange, overgrown children. Above us I could feel the gray sky rushing westward.

She took off her blue coat.

Under her coat she was in a maroon dress. I imagined it was a knit dress, of fine quality. For a split second she looked like my wife; the dark hair, the taste in clothing. Had that moment lingered I might have called out her name, but things began to happen very quickly. I knew it was my turn to take off my coat, which I placed on the chair beside me. It was time to show the woman in the maroon dress my black sweater, my gray pants. My legs felt weak, and one of them began to move with dread and with yearning and with a kind of odd grief that I believe the woman recognized, for she once again wrapped her arms around herself, and began slowly to rock from side to side. I could not look elsewhere, though my eyes hurt me as I stared.

I stepped down off of my seat and began to walk toward her. I circled over to the next section, all the while looking at her. She had not moved. And she gave no sign that she wanted me to stop my circling, no sign that she would run if I tried to join her in the yellow seats above the third-base line. She gave no sign, but I knew all the same that I was to stop there in section E, near center field. She in turn stepped down and walked to the seats above what would have been home plate, until she was once again directly across from me. I suppose I began to understand that we were dancing.

Soon enough that understanding depressed me, and I sat down. I rubbed my eyes. I did not want to dance this dance. I did not want, anymore, this intrusion of absurdity. I watched a cloud of swallows move eastward above us. I closed my eyes.

"Will it rain!" she cried out, suddenly, as if sensing my approaching despair. Her voice was small and sturdy and echoed in the stadium's chamber. "Will it rain!" she cried again.

I could not bring myself to shout back. I stood and shook my head yes. Yes, it will rain.

"Will we talk!" she cried out now, louder than her first question. "Will we sit and talk!"

And this time I wanted to cry out, louder than I have ever shouted anything in my life, "Where?" But again, I could not bring myself to shout into that gray void. I tried to shake my head yes again, but I'm not sure that I even managed to accomplish that. The distance between us was overwhelming. It pressed against me. I somehow knew that any effort of mine to cross it would prove a mockery. Any words I managed to shout would blow back into my face like paper scraps. I expected that she would soon leave the stadium, mistaking my powerlessness as rejection of her. And I would leave too, and remember her every so often as the woman in the stadium.

She did not leave. This tenacity impressed me, then moved me. I stared across at her, then once again stood up on my chair like a child. More swallows in the sky, and a huge boom of some kind shook the city, the sort I hear every day, some sort of dynamite used for construction no doubt, but at that moment I imagined it was terrorism, war. Another huge explosion. Another. Then silence.

And so we, the children on chairs, went on staring. A sprinkle of rain joined us, then stopped.

I felt the wind in my hair, and saw the wind in the woman's hair. The sun slipped out from behind a cloud. And then the woman began to slip off her maroon dress, so that I saw her white shoulders in the gray light shining, and nodded my head. She wore a white slip that also had the quality of something that glowed. The slip came down to her knees. She looked very fine in that slip in those yellow seats. Imagine her as sunshine.

For a moment I forgot my perspective of distance, and saw her as five inches tall, someone I could slip into my pocket, someone I could make a bed for in my glove compartment, someone who could drive with me everywhere. This strange thought saddened me so that sudden tears stung my eyes.

My son died two years ago, when he was thirty, in a car wreck, when he was drunk one night, or perhaps on a drug. We had been estranged for several years before this happened. Perhaps this is one reason I remember him most as a boy, a boy who loved or tolerated his father, a boy who I carried in my arms at night in the alleys of that old city, when he was small, when I could never sleep, when I felt the solidity of his body in my arms as the one certainty on this earth. Looking at the woman in her slip I remembered his mother, the night after his funeral, when our house was empty of relatives again. She was not wearing a slip, yet she stood in our bedroom with the same vulnerability of a woman wearing a slip. The best way to defend oneself against the invasion of memories is to impede their initial entry. If you've noticed. One memory gives rise to the next. You remember your wife in your bedroom the night after you bury your son, and then you are bound to remember your own abominably judgmental heart, which sat in your chest with its own cold eyes. *Pull it together,* you were thinking then. *Pull it together, you've been crying all week and I'm sick of looking at you.* My wife looked up at me in pure shock, as if she'd heard my heart, as if finally realizing the depth of my lovelessness. It is a look that pleased me at the time. I felt anointed by her vision because I knew it was finally the truth she saw, that despite the good things I have said and done, it has always been the truth, that always the innermost eyes of my heart have been cold to the suffering of others. But no, I was not, as it turns out, loveless.

I took off my sweater, my pants, and my shirt. The sun was gone. The woman across from me was naked now. I had begun to weep. I undressed the rest of the way, and dropped each article of clothing on the seats beside me. The air was cool but I did not shiver. We stood there facing each other for what seemed a good while. I could tell you she had a long neck, and a long waist, and long, heavy legs, and that all of her seemed lit up somehow. Perhaps because the air against us was cold, she began to dress, and of course I did the same. But as we dressed, we looked at one another. Finally dressed I cried out the same question she had posed. "Will we talk!"

"Where!" she shouted back, and I smiled uncontrollably.

"On the field!" I shouted. "Down on the field!"

"On the field!" she shouted back.

"Yes!"

We sat under the green plastic covering, near home plate. It rained. We may have been campers. I was filled with a kind of astonishment, a kind of fierce gratitude to find myself in the presence of this woman. She was back in her blue winter coat. We both seemed to understand that neither of us wanted to smile at what had transpired between us, or even speak of the strangeness of it, though her eyes told me she felt the same astonishment that I felt.

"Are you a baseball fan?" was the first thing she said to me. She had green eyes. Her voice was low-pitched and clear. She held her head stiffly, her neck stretched forward. She may have been fifty years old or so. She had that rare quality of seriousness, or gravity, without the predictable contemporary persona that feels compelled to mock the gravity, that laughs and skates over the seriousness.

"I was a baseball fan. As a boy, I loved the game as much as anyone. And you?"

She lowered her eyes. Before she answered I felt compelled to give her an image of myself. I interrupted her as she began to speak. I said, "I lived in Brooklyn. On summer nights I lay awake listening to Dodgers games in the dark. The room was hot and my sister in the next bed asked too many questions."

This was not the memory I meant to give her, but she looked at me as if she could see that old room, how frightened I was for reasons I couldn't name, how the windows looked out on tall buildings across the street, and sometimes a moon. She smiled.

"I slept in my underwear," I added.

"Of course you did."

We looked at each other.

"And you kept your baseball cards in shoe boxes under your bed," she said.

"Yes, I did. Lots of them."

"My husband played for the old Class D league."

"And you watched his games faithfully?"

"He was my best friend," she said. "Would you like an apple?"

She took an orange from her coat pocket.

"I mean an orange," she said, and smiled.

"Thank you," I said. She was staring at me now. Her eyes were the eyes I would've expected, cleansed with recent tears. It was strangely easy to hold her gaze.

"We could be arrested," she said, handing me the orange, which seemed brilliantly orange under that green tent of ours. "I've been here before, and a security guard once gave me a warning."

"If I get arrested, I get arrested," I said.

She smiled and lowered her eyes, then looked up at me.

"We'll leave one at a time," she said. "I'll go first. You enjoy the orange."

She slipped out from under our covering. She left without another word, and I knew not to stop her. I stayed there with the rain pounding the plastic over my head for an hour or so, ate the orange on the Astroturf, and that was the world. My head hummed with a kind of light. I said the name of my son and the name of my wife. This became a kind of prayer. I can't explain it.

I finally got up and walked out of the stadium. I climbed the fence, and walked back to my car, and drove on, listening to the radio. And for a while after this, I allowed every word that every person said, every random face lost and alone in a crowd, to somehow penetrate my heart with stabs of light.

Embraced

It was the month Aileen's parents separated, when her mother said to her, "Just call me Roseen," and her grandmother, who lived with them, said, "Then you might as well call me Belle."

They said it in the car on the way to Jersey. They said it out of the blue, as they rounded the top of the Delaware Memorial Bridge at dusk, the sky a wild flame. It was early summertime, many years ago, and Carole King on the radio sang "So Far Away." It broke Aileen's eleven-year-old heart every time she heard it.

"We got our whole lives in front of us," Roseen said at the wheel.

"And this time we'll avoid the slithery and banal," said Belle.

"The slithery and banal can kiss my ass," Roseen joked back.

Aileen wished her mother wouldn't say "ass."

♪

When they got to Wildwood, Aileen was relieved to soon find other Catholic girls like herself, who wanted to dress up as nuns and have May processions (even in July) or mock funerals, or play Saints—a game where one girl stood against the wall getting pebbles thrown at her by the other girls—or Communion, where they broke Nilla Wafers and served up the hosts to each other's tongues, or Confession, where you got in a dark closet and told your fake sins, the more outrageous the better. These girls, Kathleen and Margaret and Deirdre and Marie, all claimed to have seen the Virgin come out of the sea one night. Aileen thought this was thrilling, and made the mistake of mentioning it to Roseen. "Honey, Mary wouldn't be caught dead in *Wildwood*. She goes to places like Lourdes over in Europe if she goes anywhere."

By then Roseen and Belle were tired maids, cleaning out rented houses so the next group of tourists could move in. Belle would start to tell Aileen a story about what slobs people were, and Roseen would hush her, saying Aileen didn't need to know the grit. Roseen, instead, told Aileen how one of the realtors tipped her fifty bucks for having good legs.

After they cleaned, they'd come home for drinks. It was dusk, and the floor lamp was on in the corner of the cottage living room.

"Care for some wine?" Roseen said to Aileen one night.

"I'm only eleven!" Aileen protested.

"In some of the best foreign countries children drink all the time."

Aileen crossed her arms. She was tired and sunburned. She'd run on the beach all day, eating peanut butter sandwiches filled with sand. "This isn't a foreign country," she said.

Roseen poured Belle and herself some wine, and sighed.

"If you don't watch out, Aileen, you'll end up like Ada the Fringer."

Aileen refused to ask who Ada the Fringer was. It would be several years before she discovered Ada was an example of the wallflower in what had been Roseen's high school home-economics textbook. Ada the Fringer sat on the sidelines in drab clothing with bad posture, and never smiled.

"You need to loosen up a little, that's all," Roseen persisted. Belle in a corner chair had her head back, her eyes closed.

"Leave her be," she said. "Get the poor kid some Kool-Aid."

"Yum yum," Roseen said, but went and got Aileen a cup of Kool-Aid so she could join in on the evening toast.

Their ritual: first they toasted to something abstract like world peace or the future; then they toasted a person. You had to be quick and shout out a name all at once so they clashed in the air.

"To Betty Grable!"

"To Jackie O!"

"To Dred Scott!"

And the summer would soften into late August, the darkness falling earlier, a slight chill in the air, the tourists growing scarce and finally the town emptying so the real people could get on with their lives.

And they were real people now, when for years they'd been "shoe boxers," coming down to the beach for a long day, using the public showers, or mere renters for a week in The Sands motel. Now they could say of the tourists, "I thought they'd never leave" and "They get louder and more demanding every year."

Aileen attended a new school, Immaculate Heart by the Sea, and got a job all her own, sweeping the theater on the boardwalk every Sunday afternoon, the beautiful deserted boardwalk that ran parallel to the ocean, ghostly and abandoned in the wavering winter light, amusement rides closed down or hauled away, shooting galleries boarded up, and only a few bars, some fry joints, the bingo hall, and the Apollo movie theater left open for locals. Aileen loved her job. She dusted maroon velvet seats, swept up the crushed popcorn, cigarette butts, candy wrappers, cups, and once a mortifying beige bra she had to hide from the manager, Shillone, who was a magician and considered his theater job a measly hobby. While Aileen swept in the dingy light, Shillone worked in the high-ceilinged lobby counting money on the glass counter, half watching a church service on a black-and-white TV so he could ridicule it.

Aileen had already been to early mass at John the Divine's, sitting near the votive candles with the old people hunched in dark coats. Belle and Roseen after a morning of coffee and cigarettes in pastel housecoats at the kitchen table would make it to noon mass (the noon mass priest was better looking) in heels and hats and flowery dresses. They'd leave before the closing hymn to beat the crowd. "We're in Sin City," they'd agree from behind the netted cages of their hats, the shadows of the nets delicate and dark on their faces.

"Sister Ignatious said without the benediction it doesn't count," Aileen warned.

"You tell Sister to go take a flying leap," Roseen said and laughed.

"Fine, end up in purgatory, see what I care!"

"Oh Aileen, you don't really believe all that crap, do you?"

Once after work, Shillone showed Aileen his room above the theater. It was barren looking, the intense order of it sad, somehow. He had a cot in the corner with a green blanket tucked tightly over white sheets that were turned down perfectly with a stiff, ironed look. A black-and-white photo of Ava Gardner sat framed on his bureau and was signed "You're a Touch of Venus, Baby!—Ava."

One large window looked out at the ocean.

"So now you know how a real magician lives," Shillone said. He watched her closely as she gazed around the room. Before she left he said, "Wait, you ain't seen the closet!" He opened the door and a strong smell of cedar emerged as he pulled down the lightbulb chain. The deep closet was a little library, all magic books, he said. "And see that blue chest with the stars? My cape is resting in there. It can't come out until the night of a show."

Aileen nodded. Shillone took his black top hat from a high shelf and put it on his head and looked down at her. "I learned everything the hard way," he said. He walked over to the mirror and looked himself in the eye. Aileen watched him, and could see her own reflection, watching. "Anybody ever beat you? Any parent ever kick you in your sorry little stomach?"

Aileen shook her head no. Why was he asking her this?

"They can damage the solar plexus. You like my shoes?" he said.

They were strange with pointed toes, the color of bitter chocolate. She did like them and told him so.

"It's a long road that ain't got no turns," he said.

Aileen just watched him. He held his own gaze, and now his hat was tilted at an angle.

"What do you got to say for yourself?" Shillone said, still looking at his own eyes.

Aileen said, "Nothin' much." She could try to explain that she felt she'd fallen into a dream, but knew Shillone would not be prepared to listen.

"If anyone big ever tries to beat you, you kick him right here," Shillone said, his hand on his crotch. "You kick him as if your whole life depended on it, okay?"

"Okay."

"Strive to remember there's magic in the world."

"Okay."

"And all you got to *do* is learn a trade, move *away*, and never give nobody evil the time of *day* ever again."

He winked. He came over and shook her hand as if they were both a couple of businessmen.

After Shillone's Aileen ran down the beach; it was dark. She ran and thought of telling her father all about the magician and his advice and his cedar closet. She could see her father's face, struggling to look interested.

"Is that right?" he'd say. "You don't say," he'd say.

She missed the smell of him, his bristly face at night giving her a kiss. She missed her brother, Blaise, who never returned her calls these days. She clenched her eyes shut against the stars and asked the Virgin Mary to please help her get up off the sand and find her way back to the cottage.

"Now don't ever go into detail about El Greco's or Mack and them to your father," Roseen said one day when they were taking a drive.

Mack was Roseen's boss at El Greco's Beef by the Bay, where she now hostessed, and also her new romantic interest. Aileen had overheard her mother tell Belle that he was quite the Italian stallion.

"I'm not telling Daddy about Mack or anything else. If Daddy saw you and Mack he might think you lost your lid." Mack was the type to ask Aileen on the phone, "So how's that delicious mother of yours?"

"Mack's all right. He's up front."

"Might be up front but he wears too much perfume."

"Cologne, Aileen, cologne. And I don't know why I even care what your father thinks," Roseen said.

Aileen stared out the window at the marshlands, urgent and green under a wet gray sky, reeds coming to life for spring, racing in the wind as if to leave the earth and fly.

She remembered her brother's only visit, how they walked together for hours along the highway, the marshes stretched out on either side of them all the way to the horizon, making them feel unreal, dreamlike, so they'd kept looking over at each other. Blaise with dark hair in his eyes and his voice cracking with change, transistor radio in his hand. James Taylor, "You've Got a Friend." Her whole body had to brace itself against the sadness of this song whenever it came on. And really, why was it so sad anyway? What was so sad about telling someone they had a friend when they were down and troubled?

Later she'd taken Blaise to meet Shillone, but he hadn't understood how wonderful a place it was—hadn't grasped how Shillone was like some kind of strange miracle man, tucked away like a secret she'd discovered. Blaise had simply jiggled his knee and stared out the window, ignoring Shillone while Aileen talked nervously about nothing she could recall, trying hard to fill any silence. It was the first time she ever felt like Roseen—the way Roseen would orchestrate people. But it didn't work.

"He's weird," Blaise said, as they walked home. "You shouldn't go there."

"He's my friend."

Blaise shrugged and fell silent.

After he got on the bus to go back home that night, Aileen cried as the bus rolled down the road. Roseen gave her a stiff hug, patting her on the back quickly, a space between them built of fear becoming palpable, the source of it so old and complex it would never be mentioned, much less understood. And like anything with substantial roots, the space was growing. They walked down the narrow street in the dark.

"Visiting," Roseen said and sighed. "It's always a strain."

"We should all just get back together," Aileen said, though she knew the statement was ridiculous.

"Yeah, I could marry your father and his new wife-to-be," Roseen said. "Wouldn't that be a cute threesome?"

Aileen looked up at her mother's face in the dark. "Well? Wouldn't it?" Roseen said, smiling down at her.

Aileen kept walking.

"Don't you even worry," Roseen said.

The night Aileen's father decided he couldn't stay, Roseen had taken a vase and thrown it down the length of the upstairs hall. It crashed and shattered in the dark. She and Blaise had frozen in their beds, their bodies listening. It was not like all the other fights—no extended screaming or crying. Instead a dead silence filled up the house like water. And Roseen said *Bastard,* her voice choked, muffled. And then for the first time ever they heard their father cry. "I'm sorry," he said through his weeping. "I'm so sorry."

This was the memory that would rise in Aileen's throat and make her double over in a fit of coughing.

They were out for a drive one day. Going out for a ride in the car was a treat.

"You all right?" Belle said to Roseen.

"Just sittin' on top of the world kickin' the globe," said Roseen at the wheel, chain-smoking in a horsewoman's hat.

"Okay, Aunt Rita, bless her soul," said Belle, because that was what dead Aunt Rita had always said.

"Somebody sing somethin'," Roseen said, miles later, and Belle sang "Make the World Go Away."

"Not that," Roseen said.

Aileen sang "American Pie," every word, and they clapped.

Later Belle began making her lists, which was how she dealt with the past.

"Old neighbors," she'd announce out of the blue. "Sicilianos, Hydes, Tigues, Nibilitskis, Brennans, Glaziers, Keoughs. . . ."

"Colors of rooms in Forty-seventh Street house after the war," she'd say, eyes narrowing.

"Blue, blue, white, peach. . . . Hey, Roseen, was the kitchen blue after the war or had your father painted it by then?"

"Oh hell, don't ask me!"

Aileen didn't know her grandfather, though he was sometimes mentioned in a list. He'd vanished with a woman Roseen and Belle referred to as Big Ass. Anytime Aileen tried to find out about her grandfather, Roseen and Belle did imitations, contorting their faces and deepening their voices.

"It's Friday night," they'd say. "Let's stay home and read *The Encyclopedia of Common Disease*!"

"Feel my head? Am I warm? Do I look a little *wan*?"

"How 'bout the night he started screaming about his pancreas?"

"Big Ass didn't know what she was in for."

They laughed, and Aileen in the backseat waited for the silence that followed when both of them would clear their throats and turn toward separate windows.

One night Aileen overheard Roseen screaming at Belle, saying she didn't understand a thing about love, just set a terrible example. "Maybe you wanna joke your way to the grave, but I think there's more to it than this."

Belle's face caved in. Then they were crying on opposite sides of the room until Roseen said, "Leave me alone!"

Before Belle turned to leave, Aileen ran from that cracked door, exploded out of the cottage into the dark and all the way up to the ledge by the sea. It was black with creosote. She loved the smell. She breathed it in. Held her arms tight around her stomach.

Prayed to Mary. A very short but intense little prayer: *Help*.

Belle and Roseen decided to drive Aileen to the new suburb near Lititz, Pennsylvania, where her father, his new wife, and Blaise were living now.

In a public bathroom off the turnpike, Aileen watched Belle and Roseen redo their faces. Belle took cold cream and removed her eyebrows, then put them on again, arching them even higher so that Aileen wondered whether the brows were reflecting an inner state or helping to create one.

"You're overdoing it," Roseen told her.

"Last time I checked this was *my* face."

"Aileen, don't lean against that wall," Roseen said. "You don't know who's leaned there before you."

"You think the whole world's contagious!"

"You better believe it is."

"I sat down on the toilet seat without putting paper down first," Aileen said.

Roseen turned from the mirror, wide-eyed, stricken. "Tell me that's a joke," she said.

"Okay, it's a joke," Aileen lied.

Roseen turned back toward the mirror. "It damn well better be."

"It is."

"These damn lights make me look like I got one foot on the banana peel."

"You look fine," Belle said. "Pipe down."

Roseen was dabbing streaks of red onto her cheeks. Then she took out what Aileen had heard her call her foundation and applied it down either side of her nose, telling Aileen for the third time that it was a trick to make a wide nose seem narrow, a long one shorter, and she should learn the trick since it looked like Aileen's nose was already headed off in the wrong direction.

"Ask me if I give a crap," Aileen said, but she blushed and fought tears as she bent to tie her shoe.

"If you don't give a crap, nobody else will," Roseen said. "Count on that."

Aileen, for the first time, had a hermit vision then. She'd live in the mountains, dark wild hair hanging to her feet, she'd sleep in a shack flanked by dogs. One friend, who was also a hermit, would visit once a week.

"You wait, girl, in a year or so you'll be damn glad you've got a mother who knows how to bring your best face forward."

"The hell I will," Aileen said, and this made them laugh, the sound of it bouncing off the tile. Aileen stared up at them. They were like members of a cult she knew she'd have to join, eventually. She sensed the cruelty in the pleasure they took now. *Can't stay eleven forever, honey. Soon you'll be one of us.*

When they neared Haven Crest it was dark. Streetlights rained down. They circled the block like a shark.

"Not all it's cracked up to be," Roseen said, but Belle seemed mesmerized.

"Ground control to Major Belle," Roseen said.

"Hmmm."

"Just please get a load of that tacky joint over there with the drooling statues."

"Hmmm."

Aileen's father's house was big brick with black shutters, a moonlit maple in the front yard.

"I changed my mind," Aileen said. "I'll just stay in the car and drive back with you two, okay?"

"Go on," Roseen said. "And take good notes while you're there."

"It's only a few days," Belle said.

"Tell Blaise to come out and give us a hug," Roseen added.

Aileen grabbed her flowered suitcase and got out of the car. She felt them watching her walk up the path. If she stopped walking her legs would fly away from her body back to them.

Inside Aileen sat with them in the large living room, in chairs that seemed too far apart. Blaise was not home. The color TV was huge, commanding, a console, it was called. Aileen's father gave her ice cream and praised her appetite to his new wife, Joan, who wore a pantsuit and gold bracelets. She smiled politely and listened to everything said with interest so sincere it was painful.

"Wish I could eat like that and keep a figure like yours," she told Aileen, then looked quickly over at Aileen's father to see whether she'd said the right thing. Aileen had been prepared to dislike this woman, and now she wanted to rescue her.

"It'll catch up to me," she offered. "One day I'll wake up and look like Mama Cass."

It was what Roseen would've said.

It was a good thing Joan accompanied Aileen and her father to the park the next day. Having never spent time alone, they wouldn't have known what to say to each other.

They walked around the park in coats, Aileen in a pale blue stocking cap with a white tassel, a gift from Joan. "In summer there's formal gardens here," her father said. Silence followed. "That's nice," Aileen said, and Joan perked up to talk about roses. Aileen remembered Roseen saying not to tell her father about Mack and El Greco's.

He'd never even ask! He'd ask nothing! And all of Aileen's secret questions—How can you not miss Roseen? Do you think we'll ever be back together again, ever?—all these questions died in her now, and the girl who'd planned on asking seemed foolish.

"I really love pumpkin pie," Aileen said.

They drove to a bakery and bought one.

"Wanna go out and hack around?" Blaise said. It was the next morning, the day bright and clear. Aileen would remember the sky as so low and blue she could've peeled it back like fruit rind to reveal something wet and bluer. The yards connected like quilt patches, embroidered with flowers. The sun threw down ropes of light when you squinted.

A boy in a black driveway looked up from a struggling insect under a magnifying glass. "The little fucker's almost cooked," the boy said, and Blaise said the boy was Mike.

Later in the deep shadows of the woods Mike and Blaise left her by the creek, saying they'd be back in ten minutes. "We need to get something."

She sat by a rock, surrounding trees twisting in shadow and light and the voice of the creek trickling through her body. She grew tired of waiting and walked until she heard their voices falling from a tree fort.

She climbed the steps nailed to the silvery trunk, ducked in through the floor. The boys saw her head on the floor.

"Get out!" Blaise shouted.

"Aw, let her stay," Mike said, shining a flashlight on her face. She closed her eyes and boosted herself into the fort. Now Mike shined his light on the walls where women were plastered naked, legs open. "Get out, Aileen, we'll be down in a minute," Blaise said, softly, but his voice had a strange tremble. The hot pond of light moved from one body to the next. One woman was on her hands and knees with a man behind her holding a whip, another stood with clothespins on her nipples, her tongue out of her mouth.

"Whatta ya think?" Mike said, and now the light was shining between a woman's open legs.

"So what," was all she could muster.

Mike circled around the walls again with the light, and Aileen felt sick, her face blazing hot with pleasure-pain that settled between her own legs. These women were familiar somehow, they made sense somehow, but never could she have conjured them.

Later walking down a black road Blaise said, "Those pictures are no big deal, everyone has 'em, even fathers, but don't tell anyone."

"You think I care?" Aileen snapped, anger an arrow over the sorrow she felt now that Blaise was so far from her.

And the women were stuck in her mind, and would be for a long time. And so many of their faces, which she hadn't thought she'd noticed, held the expressions of small girls, pouting and startled. Like they might suddenly look down at their own bodies and ask, *When did all this happen? And where was I?*

She took a bus back to them. She stepped down off of it and Roseen lit up. "Hey, babe! We missed ya! Now tell all, we want the details."

How to explain it was a blur?

"I can't remember."

"Come on, Aileen."

She lied, made the visit up. They went to the zoo. The house was dumpy. The new wife's "a bit much." (They laughed at that.)

"What else?"

"Nothing."

"We'll ask you later."

In the car they headed home through the dark with the windows down, salt air lifting Aileen's hair while her mother described their cottage, all decorated for Easter. Not only that, but she got Aileen a new dress that would really do her justice, not to mention Easter hats for everyone, *damn I love the spring*. Roseen honked the horn to emphasize this point.

"Tell her about *her* room," said Belle, and Roseen said she's gonna die, it's fifty sweet little yellow cardboard chicks on the walls, a nickel apiece and she couldn't resist.

So weeks later at the Wildwood magic show in the Immaculate Heart by the Sea cafeteria that smelled faintly of milk, Aileen watched her own red shoes take her across the black and gray checked floor, following Roseen and Belle and her friend Marie Sysmanski all the way to the first row, where Roseen likes to sit because why not? Someone has to.

Outside it was dark, and a high window framed stars, and across the street the ocean poured itself down on the shore, and Aileen could hear it. Shillone was not yet in sight, the curtain hadn't opened, but Marie Sysmanski was so excited for the magic to begin that she held Aileen's arm, squeezing.

The yellow curtain opened and there stood Shillone, his back to the audience, tall in his purple cape with the letters of his name in bright orange across the shoulders.

The audience said, "Hi, Shillone!"

He turned around. He wore a fake handlebar mustache on either side of his narrow face like two black smiles hovering in the air. His real smile glinted white; to Aileen it looked angry.

She could hear the bustling excitement, the rising expectation reaching a high pitch all around her. But she couldn't feel it. In the darkness Shillone made a glass of water float in midair. Aileen folded her arms and heard Marie gasp. Shillone pulled rabbits out of the hat. Aileen looked over and saw Roseen and Belle consulting each other, mildly impressed.

Shillone made things vanish in the spotlight. A chair into thin air and spoons tossed high that never came down. And how mortifying when his beautiful assistant tripped onto the stage; she'd lost a spiked shoe and had to go back to retrieve it.

"This is the lovely Bonita," Shillone said, and ordered her into a box, and she was so calm as she turned her face in the spotlight to regard the audience who would watch her be sawed in half. Shillone began sawing the wood at the waist and Marie screamed "No!" and the audience laughed. Aileen squeezed her friend's hand, told her not to worry, but felt strangely angry at Marie for believing this trick.

But when the woman was sawed in half and Shillone pushed the boxes in opposite directions, her feet hanging out of one box, her head out of the other, Marie looked at Aileen, horrified and betrayed.

Then Bonita got out of the box, whole and looking bored, and Marie in confused relief said, "Hey!"

Driving home they were all quiet, listening to Marie, who babbled on about the magic, a sweet, naive little bird.

"Thank you so much!" she said before getting out of the car and racing up to her front door.

Late that night in the kitchen, somehow Roseen and Belle and Aileen ended up congregating.

They sat at the table in nightgowns; nobody could sleep.

Roseen said, "The moon's full to the bursting point."

"I can feel it," Belle said.

"Of course you can, it pulls on the tides, doesn't it? And we're eighty percent water, aren't we? And I wish someone would *tip me over and pour me out.* You know?"

Roseen got up, went to the refrigerator. "I'm hungry but I just don't know what for," she said.

And Aileen will see all of this one day, out in the night, looking in through the kitchen window, grown up in a coat. Roseen will turn around then, a woman who has suddenly walked up to the window of her body and pressed her face there. Roseen. Fiercely lonely.

Don't move.

Thank You for the Music

Leonarda, Leonarda,

Your cassette arrived yesterday, just ten days before Christmas. It was an astonishing gift; I stood on my rickety blue porch in the fog of December, facing the goats (I have two of them), tearing open the thick brown envelope, making sure not to rip through your address—as if it hadn't years ago engraved itself into my heart. But to see it there in your own handwriting (penmanship would be the better word here, since I see a child's effort in that handwriting, and a child's energy) was like seeing a glimpse of your face on a crowded train in Europe, possibly during the war. I know you're thinking "But Francine, you've never been on a crowded train, much less in Europe during the war. You're phobic in crowds and hasn't it been two years now since you've taken off your bathrobe?"

Maybe. But I've changed, Leo.

Now, I'm not saying I've been on a crowded train. Not lit-

erally. But you who despise the constraints of the literal—
why do you care? I have a lot to tell you. But first, a thank-
you for the music.

You know that I of all people understand the difficulties of
making a cassette tape. The intricate decision making that
happens when considering segues! The knowledge that
every segue is an aesthetic confession! What song should follow another—that decision reveals the emotional logic of the
moment, but doesn't it seem at the time that the moment is
everything? They say the moment *is* everything. All the
greats agree on that. But we don't grasp it. We open the cupboard and look for the sugar bowl, but our hearts are in
Yugoslavia, or just upstairs in the sock drawer, or wrapped
like a snake around the head of a man we saw standing on
the corner in his thin gray shorts.

So we miss the moment as a matter of course. But we don't
miss the moment when making a cassette tape and finding a
segue. We come alive in the moment then. And yet, it's work,
isn't it? Can you tell how roaringly touched I am that you
have made this for me?

I imagined you'd forgotten me altogether.

I remember many years ago I played you a tape I'd made
for that handsome ex–heroin addict priest I worshipped.
The tape was entitled *Bessie Smith and the Infinite Longing,*
and for reasons that have escaped me, I tried to segue
"Dominique" by the Singing Nun with Sly Stone's "It's a
Family Affair." I rubbed those songs together like sticks
that might catch fire. You listened and raised your eyebrow
and said, "You're kidding, right? You're not putting those
songs together, right?"

I blushed and said I'd planned all along to reorder it.

"You need Lou Reed's live version of 'Coney Island Baby,'"

you said. You spoke, as usual, with a certainty that seemed divine. You spoke as if your musical sensibility was a part of nature, not to be argued with. I believed that.

Each song on your tape has become for me a shelter. Even as some of the references to our past shook me to the core. "I can still hear the echo of those bitter words we said," sings Kim Richey. Let me tell you, old friend, the echo of those words is like a pet I keep in the basement, a mangy one that stalks my house at night.

That's the thing about a good tape though. It shakes you to the core, but then you go live in the songs that shake you, like those houses on stilts by the beach that outlast hurricanes. The songs protect you as they shake you, they're structural wonders with lots of rooms, they have windows, and landscapes. Do you know Jim Hall's version of "Concierto de Aranjuez"?

Speaking of landscapes! I hear that piece and I'm in Morocco, far from the fog and the goats that surround my present life. I'm at a small table outside a café in mid-afternoon, drinking, wizened, remembering love. (Want to join me?) My machine is busted or I'd send this Jim Hall version *pronto*. It's the only song I know that thrusts you into the future and kills you with the future's hard-won nostalgia simultaneously. It's one sorrowful piece of joy! A man I still love sent it through the mail. It's also about how softened your regrets might be if you could only get to Morocco and drink. I regret about one million things even though I'm reading a self-helpy book called *Regrets Can Kill You.* I'm always reading a self-helpy book and letting them insult my intelligence *because they are all true* and everything true is simple.

♫

I took off my bathrobe the day your tape came. I listened and knew my life would change. So what am I wearing now?

Let's put it this way. I look like I could be named Iris Dement. Where'd you come up with her? All these raw women are good for the world. To think through my youth the only woman I listened to (other than the Motown girls) was Laura Nyro. Stacked under my bed in obsessive order, those scratchy 45s. Can we surrey? Can we picnic? Later, at sixteen, I got some Patti Smith—the only person I ever wanted to be, as you may recall. One fall afternoon I thought I had the house to myself. My father, home early from work, walked into the room where I played air guitar, tossing my head wildly and screaming *"Gloria!"* I pretended not to see him. "What the hell's her problem?" he called down the hall to my brother.

All the other songs I liked were sung by men. I never stopped to consider it. I tried to prefer Ringo out of pity and to prove that cuteness was subjective. I slept with pictures of the Reverend Al Green tucked into my pajamas. I swung on the swing set at school and sang "Helpless, helpless, helpless, helpless." When I was eleven I wrote Neil Young several letters telling him how he and I were similar. Thanks for including "Powderfinger," by the way.

I look like I could be named Iris Dement (Yes, I know in the real world she's young with all her teeth, and pretty but that makes no dent with me.) You know how my tongue savors a good name. And Iris Dement is really the aged widow of a dead coal miner, whose imagination was born too late, who wears loud gold lamé slippers in the grocery store, as we did in our twenties, living in that microcosm of friendship where everyone around us seemed to be behind glass, like shoppers staring in on bargains they'd never buy. Let me tell you something. I put on one of those old outfits (Rhondina's thrift store finally closed, by the way) and I ventured outside feeling I could emerge into the world only because I was:

1. Armed with new name (Iris Dement)
2. Wearing gold lamé slippers like we did in our roaring twenties
3. Listening to your tape on my Walkman
4. Wearing what we used to call our ironic lounge wear

Ironic lounge wear on a middle-aged agoraphobic looked quite different than it did on the two of us when our long hair shone and boys trailed behind us. I knew this, but I was Iris Dement in that grocery store, able to buy beans and a Clark bar without succumbing to my usual fear. My hands didn't shake, I didn't imagine a wolfman was hiding behind every pillar, I thought not *once* of biological, chemical or nuclear warfare. Somehow I was stationed in my body. When it began to tremble, I simply walked right into that Nancy Griffith song about the kids who meet in Woolworth's! I walked right in through the back door of that old song, and I put on my Woolworth's uniform, and decided I was the manager.

How clearly I could see those sweet kids, Eddie and Rita, Rita behind the counter smiling and shining, Eddie pushing a mop. Did he have a cowlick? I was consumed with affection for them. I told them they should get married but not have a baby. (I'd heard the song before and knew the baby would die.) But of course being young and beautiful and in love and mere characters in a song, they just stared at me with a kind of pity. You poor dumb Woolworths manager, what do you know? I wanted to wrap my arms around them and take them home and keep them safe. The world would eat them with a fork and knife. And they'd just keep on dancing.

So I walked out of that grocery store rewinding that song, so as to stay inside it. You know this is a city of helicopters and makes me nervous. I walked home, eyes on the sidewalk, and was safe again.

I listened to that song forty times. I do this sometimes. It's like I can't stand the joy or the pain in a song, I want to play it so it won't be able to take me with it anymore, I want to play it until I'm deaf to it. Like Billie Holiday's best songs. Don't you want to play them until you're deaf? Am I the only one who ever wanted to have sex with a song?

Now let's talk about "Walkaway Joe" by Trisha Yearwood. Somehow I knew that song was what inspired you to make a tape, since *I* was that girl in that song, sixteen and stupid, my poor mother worried sick as I fell for Sunshine Lamont in his loud car, his brutal kisses, his child inside me after our second date—I hear the song and remember lying under Sunshine praying to die. Something was so wrong with me. They'd diagnose it today. They'd give me the proper prescription.

But all I had back then for medicine was the fortune of meeting you.

It was a mere four days after I walked out of Saint Jerome's Home for Unwed Mothers, my would-be son adopted by the loving couple with a good home.

Nobody in my family came to meet me. They had their own problems. I was alone. I was still bleeding from the birth. I was afraid to ask anyone if I was bleeding to death. I half hoped that I was.

I was six days away from my seventeenth birthday.

♫

I remember how you stood in the middle of that narrow city street offering me a cigarette you'd rolled yourself, saying, "It's European." Something about the way you said it, and the way you were dressed in that old black coat, caused the land to shift. I believed for a moment I'd been transported to Holland, the air suddenly strange and charged with Anne Frank, windmills, and children's wooden shoes.

I love you, I wanted to say then; it's true. That was the nature of my heart back then. But I had decorum. We were strangers, we were girls. I was quaking with the emptiness my baby left behind. But I so adored your face, your dark eyes, the way you flicked your hair back like a boy, your boots, your certainty, your invitation. "Hey. Let's take a walk."

I could only follow you, speechless.

We went through the yellow woods; I saw a child's toy—a horse head on a stick, the kind kids gallop around on, abandoned in the leaves. Together we walked out to a field and climbed a water tower. I sat beside you looking down at the shimmery world.

"Looks better from a distance, huh?" you said. "Check out the wildflowers down there."

(I can still hear you, all these years later. In case you ever have a moment where you think "nothing I've ever done in my life really matters," you can think again; taking me up there mattered, mattered like breath.)

♫

Up on the water tower, we looked down. Purple, yellow, last flowers of autumn. Red leaves flying like tiny carpets. You rolled a smoke. Smiled at me with eyes so kind they seemed more dog than human. Held my hand, just like we were six. I was filling up with you, Leonarda. It was as if you'd begun replacing the baby I'd handed over to the woman in the yellow scarf who had said, "Thank you so very much, you have no idea what this means!"

"I think I have a pretty good idea what it means," I'd said, groggy from some pain medication they'd given me. The baby looked at me when I said that.

Up there on that water tower, on your purple transistor radio given to you by your mother when you were twelve, we heard the song "If You Don't Know Me by Now" and you said, "This song is so great it makes me want to fly off this tower!" You stood up and flapped your arms. You howled with pleasure into the sky of autumn geese. I sat smiling, terrified. "Please sit down."

You laughed at me. "I'm right here. I'm not going anywhere."

In a plaid thermos you had whiskey and we sipped and floated in the clouds and *if you don't know me by now, you will never ever ever know me,* and I said, um, I, um, and you said, What? and I said, Nothing and you said, Come on, stranger, spit it out. But words failed me. I needed a song to explain. And I wasn't a musician. If I'd been born a musician, I'd never have had the problems I've had. I believe that. God gave me the heart of a musician without the talent, maybe just to see what would happen. Satisfied, God?

♫

Against the sky that day with you I just listened and felt the absence of the little boy who'd kicked me so hard, wanting out, wanting to meet me. He ran his eyes over my face as we said good-bye. I can sometimes touch my face and feel the trail his eyes left when he did his looking.

I always thought if I'd met you *before* I'd given that baby up, you'd have found us a way to keep him.

We'd have lived, the three of us, in that shack you found down in Matson Run.

We'd have taught him all the good songs, he'd have turned into the kind of DJ who understands that "Unsatisfied" by the Replacements is the real national anthem. Not just for the words but for the raw pain in that singer's voice.

I do wonder if he'll ever try to find me.

I do think if he did, I'd dress up like another kind of person altogether, and pretend I was a musicologist, so he didn't have to feel his biology like a dark shadow.

So I play this tape and feel you're still beside me, up on that tower where we began, and still I feel music can remake the world.

Didn't Otis Redding come on next that day?

Listening now for a moment I feel six days away from seventeen again.

A tape will come your way sooner than you think. I'm getting a job in a market. I can do it. I can do many things with music like this on my head.

Until then, don't judge me. My falling to pieces back then was not due to a bad attitude. Please believe in things like biochemistry, or maybe even the soul.

Will you visit me?

Don't pity me because I have no husband with a sailboat, no membership to a country club. (I sort of can't believe you do.) I hope he's deeply kind.

I'm writing a book about America.

Don't pity anyone. You just don't know. Maybe they feed stray cats. Maybe feeding stray cats gives them more pleasure than you can imagine, not to mention the pleasure the cats get. Perhaps a child with an overworked mother eats tomato soup with them four times a week. This child, Bernadette Opal Greer, who is mildly retarded and gets teased on the bus, this child whose sloppy face will get her exactly nowhere, this child knocks on my door late at night three or four times a week, just so I can put on her favorite song, Marvin's "Mercy Mercy Me." She listens and watches the goats in the backyard, who in the darkness are curled up asleep. Upon her face is light that nobody could ever capture. See what I mean?

I will always love you.

Francine

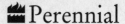 Perennial

Books by Jane McCafferty:

THANK YOU FOR THE MUSIC
Stories
ISBN 0-06-056453-9 (paperback)

In fourteen original stories, Jane McCafferty illuminates modern life, weaving her love of music throughout the lives and stories of her characters. From two middle-aged strangers who meet in an empty baseball stadium during a rainstorm, to a twenty-three-year-old man who brings his sixty-two-year-old wife home to meet his parents, to a young couple who live next door to an unemployed clown and his wife, these stories are at once unexpected and enthralling.

ONE HEART
A Novel
ISBN 0-06-109757-8 (paperback)

This inspiring debut novel from this multi-award-winning author recounts the lives of two sisters whose experiences often separate them, but whose love for one another is complicated and deepened over a lifetime.

"Told in direct, plain-spoken language, Jane McCafferty's first novel gathers genuine emotional depth." —*New York Times Book Review*

Available wherever books are sold, or call 1-800-331-3761 to order.